La Mollie and the King of Tears

La Mollie and the King of Tears

A Novel

Arturo Islas

Edited with an Afterword by Paul Skenazy

University of New Mexico Press • Albuquerque

The characters and events in this novel are fictitious. Any similarity between them and real persons, living or dead, is coincidental.

Printed in the United States of America.

Library of Congress Cataloging-in-Publication Data

Islas, Arturo, 1938-

La Mollie and the king of tears : a novel / Arturo Islas; afterword by Paul Skenazy.

     p. cm.

ISBN 0-8263-1732-4

I.   Title.

PS3559.S44M65   1996

813'.54—dc20   96-4423

     CIP

*For my students
and colleagues*

Contents

La Mollie and the King of Tears

R. O, wilt thou leave me so unsatisfied?

J. What satisfaction canst thou have tonight?

R. The exchange of love's faithful vow for mine.

J. I gave thee mine before thou didst request it;
And yet I would it were to give again.

R. Wouldst thou withdraw it? For what purpose, love?

J. But to be frank, and give it thee again.
And yet I wish but for the thing I have.
My bounty is as boundless as the sea,
My love is deep: the more I give to thee,
The more I have, for both are infinite.

WILLIAM SHAKESPEARE
Romeo and Juliet, Act II, Scene 2

"Who goes there? hankering, gross, mystical, nude . . ."

WALT WHITMAN

[CHAPTER I]

At the Movies

San Francisco, 1973

I shoulda told la Mollie I'd be back to her place right after the gig. But I knew she wouldn't believe me, specially cause we were playing at Big Eddie's, this sleazebag jazz joint in the Mission close to where my old girlfriend Sonia lives. But after them shots, man, all I wanted to do was drag this plaster leg of mine back to la Mollie so she could touch it with those magic hands of hers and make the hurt go away. Instead, here I am back in this emergency room waiting to hear if I'm ever gonna feel her fingers on me again.

All morning, la Mollie kept talking about some comet and the end of the world. Right in the middle of my giving it to her the way Rhett gives it to Scarlett the night he lugs her up them red velvet stairs after almost crushing her skull between his hands, la Mollie says, "It's the end of the world!" And I'm saying, "Oh yeah, baby," and she says, "Not this, stupid," ruining my concentration and turning me into that pansy Ashley Wilkes. I hate it when she does that, man.

"Kahoutek," she says, letting it slide out like a wet noodle.

"Ka-who-what?" I ask her.

"Kahoutek! Kahoutek!" she screams like I'm deaf. "It's a comet the Russians discovered and it's coming tomorrow. Don't you know nothing, Louie?"

Of course, she says "anything" cause la Mollie's been to college and talks English real good—not like me—and

3

she gets a big kick outta correcting me in front of her big-shot Anglo friends. She's got family in San Francisco, la Mollie, let me tell you. They're so famous, I can't even say her last name cause if she comes to, like she's gotta, and finds out I'd let some stranger know who she was and it was on tape and all, she'd chew me out and leave my bones drying in the desert.

I seen you got that tape recorder going, man. Louie Mendoza—that's me—don't miss nothing. Too bad you ain't got no TV camera so's I could be famous all over town. This ain't exactly the place I'd choose to make my debut, but what the hell. You can't help it if you're just a professor from some JC like San Cilantro and we're talking in this bloody emergency room instead of some fancy studio. Hey, I love cilantro. My mom used to put it in everything, even ice cream.

What I don't get is what *you're* doing here. It's weird to me, man, someone coming down to some bodyshop for the maimed and hopeless carrying a hernia's load of tapes and machines and all like a burro. I mean, I'm here cause I gotta be, and the second la Mollie walks through them double doors I'm gonna be gone. I wouldn't be caught dead sitting around here with these creeps if I didn't have to. But you like it, don't you, grabbing people and winding their woes onto your machines so you can listen to em again and again and write about em. Strange way to make a buck, man. I guess we all do what we gotta do.

With all them connections going for her, who'd have thought she'd end up in the emergency room at San Francisco General with a Mex-Tex Chicano with a gimpy leg the only person in the whole world who noticed? La Mollie comes from another world, man, and she didn't get born to bleed out her brains in this death hole. Her family goes way back, all the way to the Mayflower, she's always letting me know. How they got out here ain't real clear to me or her, but they're important, let me tell you.

La Mollie likes to say her great-great-great-great-great-grandmother was an Irish whore in London who picked God up off the streets and married a Puritan minister. The rest is history. When she gets into her guru act, la Mollie says she's a reincarnation of that whore. She sure acts like it sometimes, let me tell you, and all I can do is thank Miss Whatever-Her-Name-Was across the centuries for passing down some of them tricks la Mollie does in bed. I bet it was great-grandma talking the last time la Mollie and me hit the stars together, when she said in a real gravelly voice like Bacall teaching Bogart how to whistle, "If you keep that up, I'm gonna lose it, baby." That's all it took for both of us to orbit in paradise.

Me, I'm from El Chuco, man, from when the barrio was the barrio in South El Paso near the old Santa Fe Bridge that was our tie to Mexico. I was born next to that bridge almost forty years ago, though I know I don't look it. Everyone thinks I'm ten or fifteen years younger. You did, didn't you? La Mollie's always saying how much she wishes she had my skin. It's that Yaqui Indian blood of mine—skin for a lifetime, man—tough, smooth, ready. The sun don't wrinkle it. It sandblasts it new every single day. Ever hear of a Yaqui needing a facelift?

I came into the world in one of them projects near the river cause my old man didn't have no money for no hospital room and my mom refused to go to that rabbit hutch, St. James Infirmary, where the Mexican women went to have their kids. My mom said she didn't wanna have to tell no intern what to do, it was already painful enough doing it.

When I was in that where-do-babies-come-from stage, my dad liked to kid me and say that they found me under the Santa Fe Bridge. "You were washed up by the Rio Grande," my old man would tell me in his Mexican Spanish. Real serious, he liked to add, "We don't remember which side." Then my mom and him would look at each other in a sexy way and laugh and laugh. Well, I knew I wasn't no wetback Moses, so I used to look right back at my mom and say, "That sure is some bridge," cause I knew already where babies came from and just wanted to make her blush. She had this beautiful round Olmec face and when it got all red, she looked just like a pomegranate.

Her name was Praxedis but the whole neighborhood called her la Pixie cause she was always running around doing things for people like some fairy godmother on speed. Now, I think she really musta been on something cause she died so young, keeled right over the washboard into the tin tub of dirty diapers she was washing for Chula Gómez whose baby was born backwards. We called him la Nalga and I blamed him for giving my mom a heart attack. I cried for weeks and weeks cause I missed her so much. La Pixie was the old barrio's bridge to magic. If you were dying and wanted to see an elephant—a real one from Africa—she'd make it happen.

When I was ten years old, I started walking across the Santa Fe Bridge with my buddies. We stood around on the main drag acting like poor kids from Juárez and collecting enough money from the gringo tourists to go into anyplace that let us, day or night. We liked Curley's Club the best cause Don Manuel Santos was the greatest vibes player in the cosmos. He'd sit us down on the floor right next to

6

him, where I could feel the vibrations come up through my body. That old blind man's music put me into a trance and I always stayed the longest, sometimes til three in the morning. I learned more about music from him than anyone since. He always wore the same dark-brown suit and clean white shirt with no tie and the collar on the outside of the jacket even on the hottest nights. That collar was so white, it threw a glow up into his face that made him look like a visitor from outer space. To me, Don Manuel was one of the angels. He never took off his sunglasses so I never seen what happened to his eyes.

When I listened to him, I found out that music had to come outta the darkness inside and that if you were for real, you could change it into light no matter what you played. But the best part of all was when you felt your music was making other people shine. Old Don Manuel could do that even if he couldn't see nothing or nobody. Once, after he played his version of *In the Mood* that made even the toughest, crustiest stripper in the place—her name was Cassandra and she was on a break from her routine at the Waikiki #2 across the alley—get up and dance, I told him that I wished he could see what a fantastic effect he was having on everybody. He said he didn't wanna see, that it was almost too much for him just to feel it, and could I please go get him another beer? In those days, if you were tall enough to put a dime on the counter, you got a beer, no questions asked. On my way through the crowd, I was glad he couldn't see, cause Cassandra was giving everybody the finger and putting the customers' eyeglasses into her G-string. Her pimp, Romero Fasso, was snake-smiling behind her and telling the scumbags to be sure and wash their specs with alcohol or they'd go blind, ha, ha, ha.

Later, my buddies and me spent time at the Kentucky Club, where you could get five whiskey sours made the right way with real Mexican limes for only a dollar. By then, old Don Manuel had been assumed into heaven with his vibes and Curley's had closed down. We were teenagers, and we'd go across the bridge to eat. For a total of a dollar-fifty, you could have a shrimp cocktail brought in that day from the Gulf, a filet mignon with a thick—and I mean *thick*—slab of bacon wrapped around it and broiled just right, and as much Dos Equis or Tecate as you could drink and still walk.

I ain't found no food that good and that cheap anywheres else. Maybe Tadich Grill here in the City when the sand dabs are fresh and the cook is one of the old-timers in a good mood. But I can't afford no Tadich's except maybe once a month with la Mollie. And these days, the places she likes, you can forget about em. She's into carrots and lettuce and beans, man, the kind that are hand grown and cost a dollar-fifty a leaf. I keep warning her that you are what you eat. "Well, I'd rather be kale than chicken liver," she says in a real prissy Jean Arthur voice and lifts up her dress to fix her pantyhose. Man, just the click of her high heels makes me hard.

Now, no one walks across that old bridge except the people from Juárez on their way to pick cotton or be gardeners or maids for the citizens of the U.S.A. And the main street where all the clubs used to be is one long liquor store. The last time I was in El Chuco, the barrio was a big suburb way out on the east side where everybody's a Chicano or pretending not to be. Some of em even go away to college on scholarships now. But I guess you know that already, where you're from. You ever teach any of those reformed terrorists?

8

A coupla months ago when I was playing a gig down at Stanford I ran into one who was acting like Mario from the barrio and I was laughing my ass off. He reminded me of that motherkiller la Nalga cause of the way he was strutting around, his buns wrapped up in skintight pants. At the break, I asked him where he was from and real Gilbert Roland, like his lips don't open too good, he says, "El Paso." And when I say, "Oh, you mean El Chuco," he looks at me like I'm from another world and walks away all puffy in his military shirt and I'm wondering what war has he been in? Maybe he's in one at college, who knows?

When I was a member of the Ace of Spades gang in the projects, our real school was the streets, cause what they was teaching us at la High was how to be good little obedient Messicans and stay in our place. Shit, man, what did them Puritans mean to me? I always felt more like the Indians. And I never even liked turkey.

Like once our English teacher—Miss Leila P. Harper—took us to see a Shakespeare play at the local college. She spent over a month getting us ready to understand tragedy, even when right from the first, after she told us that most everybody dies or goes crazy in a tragedy and there ain't nothing the characters can do about it, I raised my hand and said, "You mean like in the projects, Miss Harper?" Everybody else laughed, but she don't say nothing and just looks at me the way them old-maid teachers do and goes right on talking about Hamlet and Macbeth and them other court dudes like they know something we don't.

Hamlet, man. You know, I still don't understand the guy but I finally decided that the whole play is Shakespeare's version of *High Noon* with a big swordout stead of a shootout at the end. Only it takes even longer for Hamlet to get there than for Gary Cooper to do what he's gotta do. I never knew no guy out for revenge who talked as much as Hamlet. He's the Prince, right? And he can have it all just by killing the jerk who murdered his old man and is now making it with his old lady. She's something else, man, and I won't even get started on her, though right now I'm thinking that's maybe why the guy talks so much—to keep from thinking about her. Anyways, stead of killing the dude everybody knows is guilty, poor pitiful Hamlet puts it off and puts it off, boring everybody but Miss Harper to death, driving his girlfriend bananas—what she saw in the guy, I'll never know—and accidentally killing *her* old man *and* his own mother before he gets to the creep that started it all. Then he dies in the arms of his best friend, who just sorta hangs around the castle with nothing to do til the end. But he don't finally hang up his spurs without a coupla more choice comments about life and people that we have to memorize or get kept after school by Miss Harper, Shakespeare's slave driver.

Oh, I forgot, he also makes his girlfriend's brother bite the dust. I can't ever thinka the dude's name cause he reminded me too much of Lencho González, one of the guys I couldn't stand in the Fatherless Gang, our big rivals for control of the projects. And poor little Ophelia, man, she floats down a river and drowns, the first wetback in the history of the English language. Guess Miss Harper was right. Shakespeare knew about everything.

I started calling Shakespeare the "to-be-or-not-to-be-that-is-the-problem" man just to make my buddies laugh and that's when they started calling me "Chakespeare Louie." Then, just when I get this Shakespeare dude pegged, Miss Harper throws us another curve and makes us memorize the "tomorrow and tomorrow and tomorrow" speech from *Macbeth,* which is the play we gotta go see at that college. The first time she read that speech to us, I thought she was saying "tomato" with a English accent and it made me thinka all these killer tomatoes on the loose.

"What are you grinning about, Mr. Mendoza?" she asked and gave me one of her razor-blade looks. She told us to imagine what Macbeth must be feeling when he says those lines. They come right after the poor loser gets told that his old lady is no longer among the living cause she couldn't wash her hands.

Up til then, I got a big kick outta the witches and I wanted to see the play. I kept thinking how it was like the gang wars in the barrio and how come they were talking about em in such hard-to-understand language? Turf was turf, man, and you better protect your own is how we felt about it. And if you were gonna take over somebody else's territory, you oughta be ready for the consequences.

Well, there we all were, sitting there in this auditorium watching *Macbeth*—four English classes from the "disadvantaged" school district plus other kids from the "privileged" side of town—and waiting to hear this famous speech. Then from outta nowhere, this string-bean college guy dressed in long dark-purple underwear and carrying a cardboard spear that was wilting at the top walks up to Macbeth and says in the biggest Texas accent you ever heard, "The Kuh-ween, m'loard, is day-ed." We laughed so hard I thought we were all, even the girls, gonna pee in our pants. Even the guy playing the Thane of Condor started laughing and pretended to strangle the string-bean dude in purple.

For weeks after, we drove Miss Harper crazy by going up to her desk pretending we were gonna ask a question and then announcing to her in all kindsa diffrent accents that Lady Macbeth had croaked. My favorite was Dolores Conrad's. She was one of the three black students in the whole school and very respected by any of the *cholas* who tried to mess with her. In fact, the *cholas* made her an honorary member of their club—the Darling Dears—after she went up to Miss Harper, waited til Leila P. noticed she was there and, making her eyes all wide and bug-like the way she knew white people thought black people always looked, said real slow, "Mizz Macbeth, she dead." I almost died laughing and I gave Dolores a big smile and wink when she passed by my desk on the way back to hers. I felt like giving her a big hug, too, but I didn't cause I knew what the guys would do to me if I did.

Now, whenever I hear anyone ask, "Why can't they learn to speak English?" specially if they say it with a Texas accent, I think about *Macbeth* and Miss Harper and wonder how come some accents are okay and some ain't. You know, I shoulda asked Miss Harper just so's I could see her squirm. Do you have any idea? You go around with your tape recorder asking people to talk. And you sit out your nights in morgue supply shops like this to pick up an accent here and an accent there to study em—that's what you told me, right? So why're some better than others, do you think? Why'd you have to come here and hitch up with me is what I wanna know. And what're you gonna do with them tapes? You know there's these tribes and stuff where they think you steal their souls if you take pictures of em? What about voices, you ever think of that? What happens to the tongue on one of them reels? Nothing personal, man, I just want to know what you're doing all this for and what you think of us all the time you're listening to us and writing about us.

Whatever it is, it's okay cause I gotta talk to somebody right now and I know you're at least gonna stick around awhile.

You know, while I been letting you in on my life, I just been thinking how so far it's sorta like a two-act play. The first act's a tragedy, sadder than *Hamlet* cause I weren't no prince, and the second is a real crazy shoot-em-up comedy with a big black hole in the middle of it. Both acts are a lot more interesting than anything old Shakespeare ever put into words, words, and more words, man, I can tell you.

But I can't talk too much about the first part cause it makes me real loco and all I wanna do is start to drink again. That first act is all about my life in El Chuco and how I had to marry Teresa Morales cause she got pregnant on me when we was sophomores, man. And it's about our daughter Evelina, born two months early and dead fifteen years later. It's also about the time I was in Korea and in a coupla V.A. hospitals right after. And about how I went back to El Chuco and then left it behind me like a man crawling away from a car wreck he knows was his fault.

I don't feel too good about that, let me tell you. I coulda stayed by the wreck like a dog that don't know no better, sniffing around for what was left of the bodies after the crash. Or I coulda done what I did and walk away, start learning how to drive more careful and begin a new life somewheres else. Hell, man, part of me is American, I admit it. I can forget the past and think positive about the future when I gotta. The Mexican part of me don't like it, but that's tough. What the past does to Mexicans is just as bad as what the future does to gringos. It's just two sides of the same craziness to be anywhere except where you are.

I got to San Francisco cause of Evelina. Right from the day she was born, there was something wrong with her cause

13

she hardly never blinked or made no sound, even when she cried. It was weird, man. Her silence made me feel all hollow and empty. It wasn't like the quiet of the desert, which I can hear and sends me right into Buddhaland. Evelina's silence was like in the tombs of mummies you never wanna meet, it really was, like she was wrapped up in that scummy gauze all the way up to her nose. Did you know that when King Tut and his buddies were turned into eternal dolls, the mummy makers sucked out their brains through their noses? Think about that, man, and you'll understand how bad I felt for Evelina. She could move and all, but she was bound up forever in some awful way we couldn't never figure out.

Teresa and me, we couldn't afford no specialist, so we kept taking her from clinic to clinic. We even took her to a *curandera* out in the desert. She took one look at Evelina, bowed like she was worshipping some god we didn't know about, and told us we had been blessed. The young doctors at the clinics kept us dancing back and forth, back and forth. That's when I started to get real familiar with hospital waiting rooms.

Why do you think they make em all like this, with the same ugly linoleum and pukey green color on the walls? I hate that color, man. And the smell—it's enough to make you sick, even when you're not. You know you're getting some killer disease inside you every time you take a breath. How do you stay healthy, man, with all the time you say you spend here? And the lights—they turn everybody into creatures from the crypt. You can die waiting for someone to see you and then die again waiting for someone else to tell you what's wrong with you or someone you love. And half the time, man, they don't even know. Every time I get into a place like this I think I'm never gonna get out.

14

Anyways, we kept going all over trying and trying to find out what was wrong with Evelina, but she never said no word we could understand. She just looked and looked at us with them dreamy dark eyes, weeping without a sound like some whacked-out Mexican Madonna on downers. Teresa kept telling me there was something wrong with Evelina's eyes, and I kept telling her that Evelina could see and that there was something wrong with her tongue and that's how come she couldn't talk, and all the doctors kept saying there was nothing wrong with her at all. Teresa and I would leave all them clinics and yell at each other the way we wanted to yell at the doctors, like maybe Evelina would come out of it and interrupt us if we just screamed loud enough. But it didn't do no good, man, none of it, not the screaming or the clinics or the *curandera*. Whatever I done about walking away, though, it wasn't cause of Teresa I left, man, you gotta understand that. She loved Evelina least as much as I did and done everything she could to keep us all together. She even made us move out to a new parish that was gonna get dedicated to Santa Lucía, the patron saint of the blind. My buddy Manitas de Oro, the great Chicano sculptor—you heard of him, ain't you, man?—did this statue of the little saint holding her eyeballs and every-thing, and Teresa would take Evelina there every Sunday and on the way outta church put her face down gently to touch them eyeballs, praying for some miracle.

That was my real crazy period and I drank all the time. Teresa and Manitas tried everything to get me to stop. But even that sweet little body of Teresa's didn't help. I'd come in maybe three or four in the morning and see her lying there under the covers, her face so quiet, her mouth so soft, and I couldn't even undo the buttons of my shirt. I'd just turn around and leave and go over to Manitas' house, where the back door was always open for me and a blanket was waiting on the couch. It was like I wanted to swallow my pain and Evelina's in each glass, man, and I couldn't do neither, and then all I could do was drink—morning, noon, and night—staring at the walls and trying to see what Evelina was seeing so's I could comfort her. It didn't work.

Man, I used to get so drunk. There was this toady old tree out in the yard that for some reason made me mad just looking at it. It was all bent outta shape like Quasimodo. Sometimes I could barely get over to it, but I hated it so much I'd beat up on it and tear off its bark and throw up all over it. You know, I don't even know how that tree kept on living, but it did. It musta been a desert tree cause anything else woulda died.

Finally, it got so bad that for about three days, Teresa and Manitas locked me up in a room with just a chair and a mat on the floor. That first night, this big fucking truck started trying to run me down. I kept running and dodging away from it in that tiny little space and banging into the walls and door and it kept coming and coming until I could hear it all around me. We went around and around like that, the roar of the engine and the headlights and me dodging outta the way. And then it turned into a giant donut and then I turned into the donut hole and then both of us were the donut. And then, after what seemed like forever, it all stopped and I was just sitting in the chair, man, and the truck and the donuts and all the noise was gone.

Then, for the first time in years, not since I was an altar boy at Our Lady of the Angels for about two weeks a long long time ago, I got down on my knees. I said, "Oh, God, please don't let it come back." For a few seconds I listened real careful, shaking cause I was so scared it would come back, but all I heard was my own heart pounding, pounding, pounding. This rosy light came into the room and poured itself inside my eyelids even with my eyes closed, and I knew what I had to do.

I got Teresa to open the door though she didn't want to cause she'd heard me screaming and yelling for all them days and nights. After I promised that I wouldn't hurt no one, she let me out and not saying nothing or even looking at her, I went outside, walked over to that hunchback tree and apologized. Teresa thought I was finally over the edge and ran to get Manitas. When they came back, they saw me hugging and kissing that tree and blubbering away like the biggest baby that ever lived. That's when Manitas knew I was gonna be all right, and he told Teresa to leave me alone and just start cooking all my favorite foods cause I was gonna be real hungry. He was right.

Manitas was always right about me, but not about Evelina. She was starting to run away all the time, til I had to stick my address and all in her wallet case she got lost. Two times in a row she came back pregnant, man, and we had to take her to some awful place across the river. I hated them trips cause I knew she was in a lotta pain, I could hear her breathing it in and out. The last time—the time that got me out of El Chuco for good—the pain beat her and there weren't no breath left. By the time I found her—in a L.A. emergency room painted the same vomit green as this one— she was already dead. She hung herself, man, in some little dive she musta crept into just to do it cause the bed wasn't never even slept in—I saw that myself when the cops took me there to get her stuff. And we never, never knew why. She couldn't tell us nothing, except through them eyes of hers. I could tell the cops thought of her as just another one of those lost kids that were dropping out all over the place then, and whoring to make do. And none of those guys she musta been with helped any more than Teresa and me, I guess. The worst punishment of all must be to hurt like that and not be able to say nothing about it. I'll never stop talking, let me tell you—but you must be starting to think that yourself.

That's when the crash came. It was like my old life went with her. Whatever had to do with Evelina—Teresa, El Chuco, the desert—it just all got sucked away under that sheet in the L.A. County Hospital. Right after I sent Evelina's body back to Teresa in the desert I was a ghost, man. I couldn't make myself get on that train and go back with her. I walked outta the depot fast, or I woulda thrown myself on the tracks. And I kept on walking all the way to this City by the Bay.

What you're seeing right now is the brand new Louie Mendoza, man. My kid brother Tomás had moved to San Francisco and gone California, you know what I mean. He was the only one I wanted to see, don't ask me why. I didn't wanna mess with his life cause I saw he was scared of what the family thought about him living with another guy. I just needed to see him. So I walked outta L.A., hitched my way up the coast til I got here, played my sax on street corners, ate when I felt like it, and slept wherever I found a place— usually with the drunks under the bridges cause they know everything about cities.

I'd never really seen the ocean, and I took my time just looking and looking at it and listening to it cause I was so empty without Evelina. I felt like I was this transparent creature with a huge heart that was all ache that other people could see, and the only time that feeling went away was when I was by the water or when I played my sax on the streets. I'd close my eyes then, not even noticing the money people were pitching into the case, just playing for myself like old Don Manuel til I couldn't play no more. Them notes got inside like nothing else, man, filling me up again and giving me back my skin so's people wouldn't see through me. Sometimes, I made up to ten bucks and then I'd treat myself to a lazy day at the beach, sit on the sand and listen to the waves til they'd start to do their work. You know, man, the ocean is like the desert, only the ocean moves and makes noise. It's a kinda noise you don't hear after awhile, but you start feeling it inside your guts like a deaf person feels music and then it starts to heal you without you even knowing it.

I got into San Francisco when all those crazy Anglo hippies, the first ones, were still putting real pure drugs in the Kool-aid and passing it out in paper cups to everybody. I never seen so many lovey-dovey people in my life. I spent time with some of them and sometimes took them to this very room. Bet I've been in more emergency tanks than you can name or wanna hear about. And here I am again. Twice in one day I been here, I tell you that yet? Only this time, it's not for me but for my old lady, la Mollie. I think I scared her to death.

La Mollie calls me her Chicanglo cause I got El Chuco written all over me but I know lots about old gringo movies so she can show me off in front of her hip pals. She tells me that my problem is that all I want to do is relive old movies stead of make new ones, and she's absolutely right. I love those old movies, man, cause they make me feel like I'm a Martian watching a world I can't never live in no matter how much I try. Imagine touching Betty Grable's legs or Ava Gardner's hair. I get turned on just thinking about it. Nowadays, the movies aren't for shit. You walk out dazed, stand outside the theater and ask yourself, "What happened?" Half the time it's like being in a hospital—you just don't know how you got there and can't figure out why you stayed.

Me, I like a movie where I can get into some of the characters and be able to tell the ending from the beginning. Once, I went to this foreign flick with la Mollie where the only thing that happened that anybody noticed, man, was a woman accidentally spilling a glass of champagne that breaks on this marble floor in slow motion. The rest of the time, everybody's just standing or walking around wearing funeral clothes in this palace in France that looked like a mortuary. La Mollie thought the clothes were "gorgeous" and everybody in her crowd couldn't stop talking about how "brilliant" the film was—her friends never go to movies like me, man, only to "films" or the "cinema." I couldn't see it. It was nothing but pure caca far as I could tell—boring isn't a good enough word.

Don't get me wrong, I like some foreign movies a lot. They used to show em at the old Yandell Theater in El Paso and the Church used to condemn em all the time. Naturally, we all went to see what was so awful. In fact, one of the best movies I ever saw—it's right up there with the very best—is a foreign flick about a little boy and his dad and how poor they are and how the dad finally has to steal a bicycle to make ends meet. Man, I cried for years thinking about that one.

When I was a kid, I almost went blind sitting in the dark for hours watching the Hollywood stars and some of the Mexican ones, too, like María Felix. They had magic, man, and they made magic. For nine cents, you could get into the old Plaza Theater—it looked like this grand Moorish castle with stars blinking on the ceiling—and sit there all day if you wanted to, seeing a movie over and over again. I saw *Gone With the Wind* for the first time when I was eight years old at the Ellanay in downtown El Paso, right across from the remains of the Old Hanging Tree. Sometimes on Saturday and Sunday afternoons, I went to three movies in a row, walking from one theater to another. There was the Wigwam, the State, the Texas Grand where they showed all the horror movies, the Crawford, and the Pershing way out in Five Points. I went to all of em. All those places are gone now, except the Pershing, and they don't even show no old movies or foreign movies at all.

And here in San Francisco everybody in la Mollie's crowd would rather go to the opera than a movie. I ain't never liked opera too much, man. But there was this one night la Mollie took me when this singer made me cry with how she was saying goodbye to her lover. She was real fat and you could tell that the snow falling all around her was fake, but somehow, her voice got to me and made me believe in her. There were tears in my eyes, I gotta admit. I kept punching the old lady sitting next to me so's she would stop snoring, and I wondered whether she'd wake up if I took one of them diamond bracelets she had on over her long gloves. The light coming from those stones was almost as bright as the light on the stage.

When you do go to a movie in this city, you wind up in one of them little cubbyholes and pay an arm and a leg to see these old movies that oughta be shown free to everybody every single day of the year. And all anyone wants to do when they see these movies is talk about what they mean. After we went to a coupla Chaplin things, one of la Mollie's friends said—I swear he said it just like this—"The Little Tramp is an example of a character who has transcended the vicissitudes of contingency and moved into the realm of the metaphysical." Existential caca, man.

When I'm with la Mollie at them Pacific Heights parties that remind me of that glass-on-the-marble flick, I sometimes act out my versions of the movies to put some life into that crowd of zombies and try to make em laugh. Or I make my accent thicker to impress her friends with how tolerant they are. You know, man, when anyone— specially another guy— treats me like a dumb Mexican cause of the way I talk, I just go ahead and act like one. That lets em stay all smug, and I can laugh at em for being so stupid. I been conning the gringos like that for years and they never catch on.

There's one of la Mollie's chums I specially can't stand. He's the kind that puts his arm around you, tells you how you're not like the other Mexicans he's met, and then starts munching on a buncha non-union grapes right in front of your face. Naturally, he's a lawyer and he's always cross-examining me like I'm on trial cause I seen some old movie and liked it and he's gonna test me to make sure I really seen the movie. It makes me wanna kick him in the teeth and the balls.

To me, man, "lawyer" and "liar" are the same word. Those dudes don't defend people—they just slobber all over the system that keeps em rich without never admitting how rotten they are. The ones in la Mollie's crowd need drugs to keep em awake during the day and drugs to go to sleep at night, and this guy is the worst of em all. Also, he thinks he's the biggest *chingón* around. *Chingón* means *fucker*, man, and you better learn to reconnize one or you won't survive in this neighborhood.

Anyways, this dude thinks he's such a Mister Know-it-all just cause he went to Harvard or someplace and he calls anyone who hasn't lived in New York City "deprived." I wish I could show you the way he says that word, like the cucumber he's sitting on has worked its way up to his throat.

So I ask him how come he don't move to New York or Boston where they talk English funnier than even in Texas. And with this look in his eye that I want to spit at, he says—get this!—that he can't live there no more cause the minorities have ruined it. Well, I wanna tell him that this whole country ain't nothing but minorities—your-orities, his-orities, her-orities—but that would be too smart for a beaner like me to think up. So I just answer his holier-than-thou look with my dumb Mexican look—like this—and he keeps on blabbing about how deprived us morons in the West are and casually flicks away some of the ashes he's dropped on the lapel of his two thousand dollar suit from Wilkes Bashford.

Guys like him don't even begin to know how deprived they are. Humility ain't in their dictionary. And this one—his name is Bruce, of course—is one of them twenty-four-hour Draculas, man, all bloated up on other people's lives cause their own are such zeroes. Bruce is always hanging around la Mollie cause they grew up together and cause she loves him "like a brother," she says. I don't know how she loves him but I see the way he looks at her. Like a real bloodsucker.

Hard not to look, man. And when she starts walking around the apartment in one of them see-through robes of hers, my brain's in meltdown. Like yesterday morning, when la Mollie deflated me with that comet? She got up, put on her pink Chinese robe, and did some stretches that had me

23

ready for my own kinda exercises. Then soon as she saw the way I was staring at her, she turned her lovely rear to my face and went downstairs to make breakfast, leaving me flat on the bed and hungry for more. She's like that, la Mollie, sometimes colder than Grace, sometimes hotter than Marilyn. So half of me thought about Grace in the shower to calm down and the other half prayed that she'd turn into Marilyn before I had to leave. I knew the chances were one in a million.

From the kitchen she hollered how do I want my eggs. I told her I like em scrambled dry with just a little brown around the edges—which she already knows, but is really busy pretending she don't hear cause she keeps banging pots and pans around like Ma Kettle. When I came down ready for love, the eggs were waiting for me all wet and runny and the toast was starting to go limp. That's when I knew she really had something on her mind, so I gave her my innocent all-American Gary-Cooper-goes-to-Washington smile and asked, "Whatsa matter, honey?"

She ignored me and said out loud to the coffee, "Comets only come around when it's the end of the world." She banged the mugs down on the table and knocked over the salt shaker. "Oh, God!" she yelled. "Now you've gone and made me spill the salt. The last time that happened, my mama had a stroke." I didn't know if she meant cause of the salt or the stupid comet, but I didn't ask her. I'm keeping my Bogart cool.

She just glared at me like Bette Davis at Joseph Cotten in that movie where she's a Mexican and hates the town where they're living. La Mollie threw the salt over her shoulder three times, ate the rest by licking the end of her finger and dabbing the grains off the table, and then just rocked back and forth, back and forth in the chair. She looked so afraid. But when I barely touched her on the hand, she jumped and acted like a snake just bit her. "How can you touch me now?" she said, stopped rocking, sipped some coffee, and then real Katharine Hepburn—like you can't argue with her or anything—she said, "The Russians know everything about space. They know what's going to happen because they are so mystical. And they don't just sit around and wait for the world to end."

I tried not to get mad, man, cause she's so fine with those freckles and creamy skin and the way the end of her nose moves when she talks. La Mollie is always getting into some cause or other. I tell her that causes ain't gonna change the world and make it better and that people are always gonna be people and mess up. And she says that all I care about is myself and that because I'm a dumb Mexican, I love my misery. I tell her that she is the cause of my misery for being such a spoiled Anglo brat. Then we don't talk to each other for a coupla days until me or her turns into Olivia de Havilland and plays sweet, mealy-mouthed Melanie Hamilton.

This time I didn't answer her right away. La Mollie and Dracula and the other rich bloodsuckers have gotten into this book about mystics in Russia and how spiritual the commies really are, more spiritual than the American mate- rialists, la Mollie says over and over just to get my goat. When Dracula and her get like this I have to laugh, cause he's making over three hundred grand a year defending the rich little drug dealers of Marin and she don't have to work cause she got a lot of money from one of her capitalist-pig grandfathers. That's what she calls him, man—I gotta tell you that Mollie don't get on too good with her family.

La Mollie's tried to off herself a coupla times, once with

some pills and once with her daddy's shotgun. But she didn't count the pills too good and just got awful sick, and the gun went off when she was loading it and warned everyone, so they just put her away somewheres for a coupla weeks. That was before she knew me and when she was still pretending she liked being daddy's girl. She's never tried nothing like that since I've been around, let me tell you, though once she tried to run me down with her Mercedes when we were coming back from a party in Los Gatos and she was drunk outta her mind. You wanna know why? Cause I kept singing the name of the town in Spanish just like it's spelled, and she kept telling me that I better learn English or she was gonna have me deported. And I reminded her that Mexicans were in this country before it was this country, and long before any of her people took it into their greedy and warped minds to murder every brown or red human being in their way. She stopped the car right in the center of a one-and-a-half lane road up in the hills where you can hear the grapes grow and said that if I didn't get my brown body outta the car, she was gonna hurl us both down the mountain. So I got outta the car, started walking down the road, and the next thing I know, she's trying to run me over, man, screaming that I don't love her and that all I ever wanna do is get away from her cause I hate her and her family and the entire United States of America. La Mollie ain't too logical.

The first time she brought up the immaculate commies was one day after lunch at Jack's with Dracula and his buddies. I said, giving her a Spencer Tracy profile, "If they're so spiritual, how come they don't believe in God?" I knew I had her there, but all she did was answer me with a Joan Crawford above-it-all look and go right on talking about

Russian history and saying that believing in God had nothing to do with nothing. And hadn't I read some guy called Dusty Ski who knew everything about the Russian soul and wrote lotsa books about it and was almost executed by a firing squad and then let go at the last second? Well, I knew about him a little cause of Sonia. I ain't told you much about her yet, have I? You just keep that tape rolling.

Sonia's mom and dad were migrant workers who ended up in Castroville, where they spent most of their lives making it the artichoke capital of the world and not getting no credit for it. They're real humble Catholic Mexican people and I dug em when I met em cause they made me thinka my own parents. They have that Indian way, man—silent, proud, all-knowing—like the rest of us ain't never gonna understand what it's all about and they already knew when they got here. Sonia's dad, he's like my dad, he's a reader, man, and he was reading one of Dusty Ski's novels when she was born and that's how come they called her Sonia. When I first met her on the dance floor of this unisex bar on the edge of Pacific Heights, I didn't believe her when she told me her name.

"You Russian?" I asked her.

"Only in my saddest moments," she says, laughing.

I was thinking about all this while la Mollie was talking to me but I ain't told her much about Sonia, let me tell you, and this ain't the time to let on that I know about them Russians when she's going at me in that know-it-all tone of hers. So I just said no, I hadn't read him, but that almost being shot would make anyone believe in God. Then I told her that all I had time to read was the newspapers since I was the one who had to work and that the Russians weren't doing too hot in them, and that most people in this country

27

thought the Russians were under the influence of the devil and were gonna start the end of the world.

"Oh, please," La Mollie said in her teacher tone of voice that reminded me of Mrs. Clark in third grade, who used to lock me in the closet cause I'd speak Spanish in class. "When are you going to stop being a dumb Mexican from El Paso, Louie? How can you possibly believe what the press in this country says about anything? There are even more lies in the newspaper than there are in the history books," she says, real Lana Turner. "I believe Fidel Castro before I believe the Pentagon." Then she gets real sarcastic cause she's just been drained of every ounce of blood in her body by that vampire attorney, "What did they do to you there?"

"Where?" I asked, falling for it.

"That hick town you're from. Were you drugged into happy obedience by lithium in the water or did they just choke every molecule of oxygen out of your brain with all that junk they spew into the air out of the world's tallest smokestack? Don't you get it, Louie? That gang life you're so proud of talking about, didn't it make you see that it's all about power? What they're doing is sucking out what little you ever knew with their chemicals and then filling you up again with their lies. Newspapers only tell you what *they* want you to know. They're like government whores out to screw you and keep you in bed nursing your tired old pecker instead of looking at the scum that runs down the sewers and ends up polluting the Rio Grande. They're poisoning everybody with lead, Louie, and then they turn around and blame the poor people across the river whenever there's a temperature inversion." I love it when Mollie gets mad and talks like that, man. She's real up on issues, la Mollie, I gotta hand it to her. And one of her favorite subjects is how everyone keeps doing what she calls blaming the victim.

"Well," I say, real nice cause I don't wanna start a fight first thing in the morning, "I don't believe what any of em say. This dumb Mexican can think for himself, honey."

When I first met her that weekend in Golden Gate Park, la Mollie was trying to finish a dissertation on the "underprivileged" along the U.S.-Mexican border so's she could get her Ph.D. in sociology from Berkeley. Well, she decided that I, Louie Mendoza, was gonna give her the inside dope on what people were really like in the towns by the Rio Grande, specially El Paso. Sorta like you, slumming to pick up some native talk, man. Ph.D. had never meant more to me than that joke about piled higher and deeper, but I was in love and just listened to her talk about the poor for hours and hours. Half the time, I just nodded and played with her hair. I didn't care what she said. I could watch her mouth forever.

Our very first argument was about how I thought people are pretty much alike anywheres if they're poor and ignored by the rich, and she said that was too obvious and too general and that I wasn't taking into account what she calls the racial and ethnic dimensions of the process. She pronounces it "die-mansions" and when she says process—which she says a lot—she says "pro-cess." I tell you, some people will do anything to make other people feel small, but I don't fall for it and say in my own way, "Jes, baby, joor rye. We're poor *and* Messican up and down the Tex-Mex border."

"That's exactly my point," she said, getting that puckery mouth that sends me into a tailspin. "It's the racial bias that concerns me in the whole pro-cess. Think of the Indians on the reservations, the blacks in Harlem and Watts, the Puerto Ricans in New York, the Chicanos in East L.A., your brothers and sisters on this side of the border. Are they poor because poverty's in their genes or because they are and have been historically exploited by white male society?" I wanna say something but she don't wait for me to answer and just goes on telling me about some famous theory of the ideology of the poor. Later, I found out it was her third dissertation on the subject cause no one version is enough for her. She's been bouncing from literary to psychological to sociological and hasn't come up with no answers, just a lotta what she calls "data" about the poor. And that's how come she said she was so excited when she met me—a real example of ethnic and racial poverty, resulting in cultural deprivation. Of course I don't know what she's talking about except the poor stuff. I think she's really excited cause she found out right away what a good lover I am, but naturally she don't wanna let on about that. I know them flashes in her eyes want more than just to pat a statistic on the head.

That first argument was pretty tame compared to the ones we've had since. It ended real nice when I told her that studies like hers weren't gonna cure the poverty of the world and that in my humble, uneducated opinion, if privileged people used all that data to figure out a way to share a little of their money, poverty might disappear. La Mollie just looked at me with those Hedy Lamarr eyes and changed the subject by licking my ear lobe.

Seems to me that sometimes la Mollie is just like the politicians and jumps from one side of an issue to another depending on what she thinks people wanna believe. And then she finds some study or expert to back her up. Mostly it don't do no good to fight with her. La Mollie's an idealist, man, and even though she don't see what it means to be poor cause she ain't never had to be, her heart's in the right place. It's just that she's trying to figure it all out with her head too much of the time, and that ain't gonna get her nowheres. She knows what's doing, La Mollie does, but she don't know what to do. She just winds up talk, talk, talking about the poor without helping em out.

Yesterday when she was going on and on about that Russian comet I started getting real mad but I didn't let on. I just told her I needed some time to myself before going to the gig in the Mission. What I was really hoping for is that she'd give the commies and their comet a rest and beg me to stick around so's we can play Deborah Kerr and Burt Lancaster all afternoon. I could feel the waves crashing over our hot, wet bodies. You know what I mean?

Instead, la Mollie started right in on Sonia with no reason at all, cause I haven't seen her for about two months and ain't said nothing about her for even longer than that. But that's when I shoulda realized that comet meant me no good. "I bet Sonia knows about the comet and I bet she believes in mysticism," was what la Mollie said in a real soft and wicked voice.

"No," I tell her. "Sonia believes in God."

"Just like a nice Mexican girl should," la Mollie says, and I feel like Cary Grant before he knocks Tracy Lord on her fancy Philadelphia cream cheese ass.

La Mollie knows that Sonia lives in the Mission by Big Eddie's. After awhile, in my best in-control Cagney-at-the-breakfast-table voice, not mad or nothing, just real even with my eyebrows level, I ask her, "Well, when did it come the last time?"

"What?" she says, buttering more toast for me real hard and punching holes in it. I hate toast with holes, man.

"That comet with the weird name." Now Cagney is starting to get mad and there's no grapefruit around.

"I don't know. About fifty years ago. Maybe a hundred," she says, kinda annoyed like it don't matter. I can tell she don't know when.

"Well, did the world end then?" I give her my Clark Gable smile.

"God, Louie, what are you talking about?" That's when she transfers the butter from the tip of her finger to the tip of her tongue, so pink and fresh I feel like I'm melting with it inside her mouth.

"You said the last time this Ka-who-tack . . ."

"Kahoutek! -tek! -tek! -tek!"

"Okay, okay. Tek, tek, tek. You said the last time it showed up, the world was supposed to end. We're still here. Look around you." And I get up and do a Montgomery Clift walk to the window, hoping she'll notice. Outside in the garden, all the hydrangeas are blooming and the tulips I planted are having an acid party thinking they're real.

La Mollie is too quiet though, so I turn around and look at her like Basil Rathbone studying a bug. She is looking at the eggs on my plate and rocking again. That rocking makes me feel like Charles Boyer and I wanna pick her up and put her on my lap and hold her in my arms. "Well," she says real soft so I can hardly hear, "maybe not *end* exactly. But I know, Louie. I feel something real bad is going to happen and that Kahoutek has something to do with it. Just you wait and see, Louie Mendoza." She pronounces it "Mendoze-uh" and now I know I want her there in my lap.

"Oh, baby," I say to her, praying she'll fling out her arms to me like Ginger Rogers to Fred Astaire in that dance where he's kept her from killing herself. "That's all superstition. Something bad happens every day." But Astaire and Rogers vanish and right in the middle of the day, there's

Evelina sitting next to la Mollie at the table, staring and staring at me with those big vacant brown eyes of hers. My Evelina, who I ain't seen for so long.

"What's the matter with you?" la Mollie says, her face halfway between funny and scared.

I can't talk, I can't move, I'm Boris Karloff on the operating table, man, looking at Evelina looking at me. Then, after awhile, it's just the sun again hitting la Mollie's hair and making it burn.

"You just wait and see, Louie," she says again.

So I shoulda known by then, what with comets and Evelina coming for breakfast, that something bad was gonna happen. Cause like every woman I've ever known who was a real woman, la Mollie is a witch—a Glenda-the-Good witch, not a Margaret Hamilton "you-and-your-little-dog-too" witch. Teresa was like that a little bit, and Evelina was, I bet, though she never could warn no one but herself about what she saw. Sonia's like that, too, only with a diffrent kinda power that I always knew was gonna protect me.

Very few guys have that power, man, we're too stuck to the ground punching it out all the time. I think guys are just drones, man, always outside the hive trying to get in so they can feel what it's like to make life. To make life, man. More than half the time, we're just buzzing around, buzzing around, being bored. I mean, look at the work most guys have to do. Even doctors and lawyers. Buzz, buzz, buzz, man, marking time til the heart attack or til someone squashes em out. Women outlive and outlove us, man, no contest. I gotta laugh when guys think that just cause of this thing between our legs we can run the world and everybody in it, specially women. And I know there are plenty of women who like to lie to guys about that. But it's the women who have the real power, man, even if they never believe that, so guys take advantage.

Face it, we guys can be fuckers. And we wanna conquer everything. I got this theory that war starts between a man's legs. Could you ever tell your dick what to do, man? It did it, whether you wanted it to or not, including just hanging there like a rag when what you wanted it to do more than anything in the world was stand at attention. And so guys start playing with substitutes. Women don't have no penis envy. Men do, and where we are is between two bunches of old farts—one bunch high on vodka and the other on old-time religion—playing mine's bigger than yours. It's real scary, man, so scary that if it weren't for women, we woulda blown ourselves to bits by now. A good woman and her power all around you like electricity, man—that's what you need to survive. And for me, music, too, cause if I didn't have that, I woulda killed myself or someone else a long, long time ago.

So there I was, staring right at la Mollie and not seeing her, even with her looking like Rita Hayworth in that movie where she comes down to earth and nothing dances the way she wants it to. But I don't tell la Mollie none of that. Instead, I say real casual like James Dean pretending he don't care one way or another, "Baby, you wanna mess around? I'm not too tired."

I knew she was gonna say "No!" cause she don't never like to make it in the daytime with the sun shining bright into the bedroom. La Mollie's real conventional about that and only really feels like it in the dark so she can pretend I'm Marlon Brando or whoever is turning her on that month. I don't mind, man, cause when I need to, I always bring her back around to me. So it knocks me out when she says

"Okay," and I tango over sideways to pick her up off the chair.

But after a coupla long kisses, she slips away and says, very Barbara Stanwyck, "Stop right there. We'll finish it up tonight. After the gig." I'm hooked in *Double Indemnity* then, man, feeling like Fred MacMurray getting took and knowing it, all helpless and telling the story into the office dictaphone thing before he drops dead. I had to sit down.

"Who's going to drive you home?" she asks, cold as Cruella De Ville.

"Tito," I tell her. "He's borrowed the van for his drums just for tonight." I'm lying cause I know that Tito can only get that little VW bug that looks like a cockaroach and ain't got no brakes. It's a certified death-mobile.

"Come on, Mollie, let's fool around," I say, feeling like Jimmy Stewart standing all hangdog in the snow.

"Tonight," she answers. "After the gig." Then she kisses me on the nose like I'm some poodle. "And I better not smell another woman on you, Louie," and she turns away from me in that put-down way she has.

Well, that got the blood outta my crotch and into my head and I grabbed her from behind, whirled her around to face me and said, better than George Raft, "Maybe Sonia will show up." I force my eyes not to blink when I see la Mollie starting to smile back at me. "Sonia ain't no Shirley Temple from the Good Ship Lollipop," I tell her, real vindictive. "She comes to where I play. She ain't scared of nothing, not even some stupid comet with a Russian name nobody can pronounce."

So it's my fault what happened cause I didn't believe la Mollie. I let her go, man, like I was dropping a tissue, grabbed my jacket and sax, and as cool as cool can be, like

I'd rehearsed that exit all my life, I walked out the back door without saying goodbye or nothing. I just left her to the Indians, man, like John Wayne on his way to the Red River with all them cows.

[CHAPTER II]

Trees

I t was only about two o'clock then but my brain was
already feeling like I'd left it out in the desert sun too
long. So I decided to walk down to the Park through the
Panhandle. It was pure San Francisco. The fog was all burned
away and the sun was hitting the leaves of the eucalyptus
so they looked like trees made outta glass chips. The smell
of salt and flowers was giving me a natural high. You ever
walk through cities where you lived for awhile when they're
like that, all smiles and shine? Man, they're like launch pads.
Every time you see something or go somewhere suddenly
you're in orbit looking at what ain't there but used to be
and still is, making you notice it all in a special way. This is
a great city for that, man, and I can't hardly take a step
without stumbling through some hole in time.

From a coupla blocks away, I could hear the kids of the
Haight and Western Addition running and hollering the way
kids do when they find a green space in the middle of con-
crete. They sounded like *cucuys* on Halloween. You know
that word—*cucuy?* Every Mexican kid grows up on it. A
cucuy's kinda like a Mexican bogey man, only lots worse, if
you ask me. I think it's an Aztec word but I can't find it in
no dictionary. Maybe it's another one of them Chicano
words that never gets written down.

When I got to Oak Street, I could see them kids weav-
ing in and out of them winos, who were just sitting and

lying around like old newspapers delivered by a maniac high on angel dust. Some of em were looking to see what was left inside their brown paper bags. Man, I remember that time in my life when a brown paper bag was all I lived for and I didn't care what kind of alcohol was in it. By the end, I was even adding lighter fluid to the Ripple so's I could stay high longer. Don't ask me how I survived that, man, cause I don't know.

Alcohol is the biggest *cucuy* of all. A real killer-diller cause it pretends to be your friend for a real long time, the kinda friend that tells you all kindsa lies. Lies like nothing's wrong and everything's okay, even when you wake up not knowing how you got where you are with your face and chest all covered with dried-up puke. And what does the alcohol *cucuy* tell you? All smiling and gentle, it tells you to have a drink and everything will be okay. And you do what it says, while all the time that *cucuy's* planning for the day you wake up and it's sitting right in the pit of your guts, man, looking like one of them stone gargoyles I seen in pictures of Notre Dame cathedral and telling you with a real hard grin, "I'm in charge now, sucker." And then there ain't nothing you can do about it. A man can ignore anything—his heart, his head, even his dick. But there ain't no way he can ignore his guts. And a *cucuy* in the gut is the second worst feeling life has to offer.

When I was a kid, *cucuys* was the one thing that scared me, cause they not only showed up when you least expected, they followed you around day and night til you got up the nerve to catch em unawares and face em in the dark. I'm a sun person, man, so what got me worst of all was expecting em to come outta the shadows in the nighttimes. You don't know about nightmares til a couple *cucuys* take over your dreams. I was always up caca creek when a *cucuy* decided I was a bad boy and needed some discipline. My brothers Tomás and Chuy and even my sister Concha used to laugh at me for being such a scaredy-cat and they stopped believing in *cucuys* way before me. I still believe in em, man, though I don't tell nobody. Maybe cause of how *cucuy* rhymes with Louie. When I run into one, I take out my sax and start playing the hell out of it til I don't feel it lurking about no more. They can't stand no beauty.

Once I done something bad to my friend Tito and I made the mistake of thinking that the *cucuy* that'd been following me around was gone. So I put my sax back in the case and walked all confident into la Mollie's bedroom while she was out shopping and without thinking or nothing, just like a damn fool human being, I look in the mirror above her dresser and I see that *cucuy* behind me giving me its gargoyle look. It was the afternoon and I was feeling brave so I turned real fast to face it but of course it disappeared. Then I looked into the mirror again and there it was, grinning away at me with all its horrible teeth showing all rotten and yellow. I could almost hear it, man, no lie, and even thought I was smelling it, a stink almost as bad as this place. I ran outta there and back to my sax faster than Superman to the rescue and I was real happy la Mollie wasn't there to see me. She don't believe in no bad spirits, man, only in bad people.

Walking through the Panhandle, I was keeping my eye on a coupla kids throwing empty pop cans at a drunk passed out under one of the great big eucalyptus trees that line the street. I walked over and stood next to him til the kids ran away. For a few seconds, I thought the old guy was dead cause I couldn't see or hear him breathe and cause he was laying flat on his back with his arms and legs stretched out like a windmill. He was wearing layers and layers of them dark and dusty clothes drunks find in alleys, you know, the kind the moths are still chomping on. Even on the hottest days, drunks are cold.

I looked at his feet and saw he had the sole of a shoe wrapped around one foot and nothing at all on the other. One hand was grabbing the grass like it was holding on to stop the whirlies and the other was palm up and wide open to the sky. He had this long salt-and-pepper beard and a flea-bitten hat on his head that looked sorta like the pictures Miss Harper showed us once of Walt Whitman, North America's answer to Shakespeare. But this old coot didn't look like he ever wrote no poem, man.

I stood over him for a long time til I was sure he was breathing regular. His feet looked so bare and helpless they made me thinka this guy that used to walk through the projects, barefoot and crazy, after thunderstorms in the desert. He'd come up on us kids splashing and jumping up and down in the mud puddles, point up at the sky like some coo-coo prophet and tell us in the deepest voice I ever heard that there was a pot of gold at the end of all them rainbows. He tried to talk us kids into going to look for it but we knew better.

Every time he said "gold," he spit out this long dark stream of tobacco juice that just missed landing on our own bare feet. We'd look at the sky and pretend we saw all kindsa rainbows. He'd watch us for awhile with his red-rimmed eyes like he was in a trance, then he'd start shaking and mumbling, and finally he'd get quiet and walk on down the street to the next buncha kids and start the same routine all over again. Later, we found out he was arrested and put away for doing something to a kid too young to know there ain't no pots of gold anywheres we could reach em. Like la Pixie said to us the day we found out the old guy got caught, "Rainbows, *si! Oro, no!*"

I learned real early that the whole world is crazy, man, specially guys. Why pretend? One pot of gold after another and always out there. It goes on forever to infinity, man. Most guys are scared to look inside, have you noticed that? And that's where the gold is, only it's too hard for em to admit it.

Even now, every time I see Judy Garland sing *Over the Rainbow* in that black and white Kansas before she gets carried away, I try not to think she was high or nothing and just listen to that pure, pure sound coming outta that small body and off I go into my own pot-of-gold trance. All this rushing after rainbows when it's the rain that counts. I cry with joy that Tlaloc and his Olmec-god buddies brought rain to the desert. Here, in San Pancho, everybody takes the rain for granted. Once in awhile, though, they have to pay their respects to the earthquake gods and the whole city trembles for a coupla days. I love them times, man. Everything vibrates, like the voltage got turned up.

The old wino wasn't vibrating but he was starting to show signs of life. I didn't want him to wake up and ask me for money and I knew that if I left some in his pocket, he would only drink it away. So while he was still yawning and before he opened his eyes, I thanked him from the bottom of my heart cause I was thinking how I could still be him but I wasn't, and I grabbed my case and walked away. I headed for the arboretum in the Park, which is where I go for peace and quiet.

I gotta tell you another sad story, man, to explain the Park, so in case I start crying, don't pay no attention. It's about my old man. He was a gardener and took care of lawns and trees in the rich people's part of El Paso in the summers. When they didn't give him too much work in the winter time, he went wherever there was a job. He traveled a lot and we hardly never saw him.

He was probably a drunk, but he was a nice one. He never beat up on la Pixie or us kids and only hurt himself. He drank mostly on weekends or when he didn't have no work and had to stick around our place in the projects with a dumb smile on his face. So even when he was there, he really wasn't there. You know what I'm saying? I know now that he drank to swallow his pride or he woulda gone nuts and started killing people cause he hated them times when he couldn't give us nothing. La Pixie knew how to handle him. "Tacho," she said—his name was Anastasio—"you go play cards and relax. We ain't gonna go hungry. My beans have more iron than steak. Look at your kids, they're strong and healthy, thank God. Now, go on and get outta my way. I got plenty a work to do here in the house." And he did what she said. She was a lioness, man, they do all the real work cause they know how.

My father was real proud he was a Mexican and told us kids, specially me cause I was the oldest boy, that we must always love our mother country cause it was part of our blood. Mexico didn't treat him no better than the U.S.A. but that don't matter, he said, cause in Mexico you were respected for what you were and not what you did.

Before we started going to the public schools, my old man taught me and the other kids in the neighborhood the capitals of all the states and countries in America. To my old man, America was this whole part of the world, not just the U.S.A. And he told us that we came from people who had great civilizations long before they were "discovered" by the European guys out for gold in what they called the New World. It was new only to them, my old man said. "History is a whore," he'd say. "She goes with whoever has the gold. Don't you believe all them lies they're gonna tell you in school." He spoke to us in his low-class Spanish, man, and angry-like, holding onto our arms tight and with little bits of spit at the edge of his lips. And when he made big statements like *"La historia es una puta,"* we listened with Chicano ears.

My favorite times was when he sat me down next to him on our old dark green sofa with a gardening book in his lap and taught me the names of plants in Spanish, English, and Latin. I could smell the alcohol on his breath but I couldn't say nothing cause I ain't never seen no one with eyes as green as him and they just held me down there next to him on the couch. He got a big kick outta the way I could pronounce some of them words and his smile made me ignore the liquor smell of his mouth. What gets me is that he was my father and he was a stranger both at the same time. I can't never figure that one out, man, but I know the greatest gift he gave me was this love I got for things that grow.

The last time we saw him was right before Christmas, nine months before I fell into the clutches of Leila P. He told us he had a job in the lower Rio Grande Valley, and that it was gonna pay real good so's we could have a real Christmas when he got back. Us kids were already real sad cause it was our first December without la Pixie and even though our Tia Irene was an okay lady, she didn't have no magic tricks up her sleeve. I was crying like a baby when he said goodbye and he don't tell me to stop.

"Look at the trees," he says to me. "They'll take care of you, Louie. You don't need no mother or father now." He kissed us all and left. When he didn't come back a month later like he said, we knew we wouldn't see him no more. Don't ask me how we knew. We just did. But I done what he told me since then.

Well, no tears this time, man, maybe cause when I was talking I was thinking how la Mollie feels my old man was a jerk for leaving us kids behind. She says no woman woulda done that and I tell her one more time that men are diffrent. She's always pretending we're all some unisex freaks and talking about the yin and the yang and how they're together in a circle. But women and guys ain't never gonna be one and the same sex. That's just life, man. It's clear to me.

"Well, not with guys like you around, Louie," she says. "You're still living in the trees."

"That's right," I say back to her. "Just like my old man told me to. And you know what, baby? I'm proud of it." Sometimes, if I'm not too mad, I ask her if she wants to swing from limb to limb with me. Mosta the time she says no.

"I still think he was a jerk to leave. Totally selfish and irresponsible." But I know she ain't talking about my dad but her old man. He's left her mom about three times, each time for some real young chick who makes it easier for him to get it up. La Mollie knows that but she don't like it too much and takes everything her filthy rich daddy does in a real personal way. Once I asked her, "Who's married to him—you or your mom?" I could tell that hit her cause she didn't give me no answer. But her look got softer so I slipped in one more comment. "Maybe your mom would be better off without him." That got her goat and she told me there ain't never been no divorces in her family and she wasn't about to let her mom be the first.

Right now, I think her mom and dad are back together but I don't know for sure cause they won't have nothing to do with la Mollie as long as I'm in the picture. I ain't even called em tonight cause I know they'd hang up the minute they heard my voice. Funny, huh? La Mollie tries to off herself when she's with them and probably wouldn't even be around right now except for me, but they don't think about that. They got a real rigid philosophy of life.

Me? I'm an eclectic, man. Since I learned I can't control nothing, not even myself sometimes, I take from here and from there whatever works. Life is a miracle and the world is loco is how I see it. I kept wanting what I couldn't have and kept trying to make all them mirages real when they weren't nothing except in my head. Now, man, when I got a beautiful woman giving me some attention and good food on the table, that's plenty for me. I ain't no intellectual. You can tell by looking, huh?

Time ain't nothing to me except a beat for my sax. I don't think there's no future, man. It's all right now and this moment is already history, so maybe the whole thing is a dream after all. I live backwards, man. I think we come from someplace else that's better but I don't know and don't care if we ever go back to it or not. I'm sitting here and your tape keeps rolling round and round and that clock up there on that pukey wall keeps turning round and round too. It all looks like it's going somewhere or adding up to something but it's not, let me tell you. I could talk to you forever, man, and I wouldn't get nowhere but here, just waiting in this hellhole not knowing what's gonna happen to my la Mollie.

Anyway, I was getting happy just walking into Golden Gate Park and telling my heart not to be so heavy. I can start smelling them trees again, man, just by talking about them. *Cucuys* don't like trees, so I never have to worry about running into em there. And then, on the grass in that open stretch between Kezar Stadium and the arboretum, here's this couple kissing and kissing just where la Mollie and me met during a love-in while the Dead were wailing away and everyone around us was flying on something unnatural in a greenish-colored sky with orange eyes floating around like stars. I'll never forget it, man.

I was living with Sonia in the Mission then. Her mother had been crying to her all week on the phone like she was ready to pour dirt over herself. She told Sonia she wasn't talking to Sonia's dad no more ever, but when Sonia asked her what was wrong, her mom only said in Spanish: "I can't. I can't tell you. Only God can know our sins." It got so bad Sonia finally had to drive down to Castroville to hold her mom's hand and tell her everything was gonna be all right.

And horny ol' Louie, prize fighter against *cucuys,* was on the prowl. I wasn't looking to get involved or nothing, man, I was just itching and scratching away like a hungry Rio Grande rat looking for sweet possum. You know what I'm talking about—you're a guy, ain't you?

Without me knowing it, my insides were searching for something I thought I stopped wanting a long time ago, and so without me planning it or nothing, I got it. My karma hit my dogma like a two-ton truck. That's a joke, man, you can laugh if you want. You don't have to look so serious all the time. That space of grass is where my life turned over and Act Two started. From nowheres la Mollie entered, gave me a look that was even hungrier than mine, and we were off and at it nonstop.

Even when we were getting down to it real serious, la Mollie and me couldn't stop laughing between the pants and the howls. It was like I was getting to make love to the whole United States of America, man. Not only that, it was letting me teach it stuff it hadn't dreamed up yet and letting me hurt it a little bit for being so mean in the past. I ain't never had anything like that.

When I got back to the Mission—I don't remember how—it was already Monday afternoon, late. I could feel every hair on my head and I couldn't barely walk. Sonia took one look at me and said, "I spend two days listening to my mother prepare herself for the everlasting fires of hell and I come home to this? You ain't touching me for ten days, creep. Not until you go to the 4th Street clinic and the results of the blood tests are back. You hear what I'm telling you, Louie?" I didn't care, man. I was in love and didn't wanna touch no one but la Mollie. It was like walking into a movie, man, all them Technicolor, star-spangled dreams that seemed to happen to everybody else but never to me.

When I first met Sonia in that unisex bar it was real diffrent. There weren't no U.S.A. about it. To me, she was pure Chicana in that low-cut black dress, black spiked heels with ankle straps—I love ankle straps, man, they give me real dirty thoughts—and no bra or panties. She'd pull up her dress just enough to tease everyone with the insides of her thighs, let her bright red fingernails linger above her cleavage just long enough to make the angels notice, and then put both hands behind her neck, still swaying like an eel in heat, to push up her long and curly very black hair so that any air left in that swamp could cool her off right where she would feel it the most. She was burning the place up, and everybody knew it, even the two fairies behind me arguing about where she came from. I wanted to tell em she was a Aztec princess but I didn't wanna give em any ideas about me. So I kept my mouth shut and just listened to the Tinkerbells.

"She's a Mexican, I tell you," said one.

47

"Puerto Rican," said the other. "Look at those lips. They're too delicate to be Mexican."

I turned to give him a dirty look but he was staring at Sonia like he wanted to be her. Meanwhile, she's still spinning her web, moving to the music like she's dancing in front of God, man, smiling like in a trance, her eyes slinky and half-shut like some Kama Sutra spirit ready to destroy the world with sex.

"She's Mexican, I tell you. I met her at a party in Marin last week. She's the most gorgeous fag hag around. Makes me think of melons and papayas in Puerto Vallarta." He said it the Anglo way—Porto Valarta. I hate it when they say it that way, man. "Let's call her melon," he says and makes the other laugh, that real fake cocktail laugh that makes me feel like punching em both to shut em up. But then he says real serious, "God, I think she's turning me on," and I tell the bartender to give the fruits some drinks on me and send a glass of champagne to the only woman on the dance floor. He knows exactly who I mean.

I was watching the cute little waiter carry the tray as high above his head as he could so the dancers'd notice him and move aside. He was about two and a half feet tall. For a coupla moments from across the room, I can see Sonia take the glass from the tray and bend down to ask Mr. Dwarf where it came from. I guess he pointed in my direction, cause the next thing I know she's gliding toward me through the crowd, glass still full, and hands it to me.

"I don't accept drinks from strangers. I buy my own and anyway, I don't like cheap champagne." She says all this in a voice that makes my shorts feel tight, with that half smile and look in her eyes that tells me that no matter what she's saying, she wants me. Only Chicanas can look at you like that and say the most insulting things to put a guy in his place, man. Chicanas and Sophia Loren. Maybe all Latin women, I don't know. But she not only got me to buy a bottle of the most expensive champagne in the place, but share it with the two fairies she was with and drive them and her home. Then she left me sitting there in the car at three A.M. wondering what happened and praying that the *cucuys* were already in slumberland cause I didn't need to deal with them too that night.

Two weeks later, me and Sonia were living together in her flat on Guerrero Street. For awhile it was like with Teresa before Evelina was born and before I got sent to Korea. We had a good hot time and we were pretty happy til I ran into la Mollie and my life took off in another direction down the yellow brick road.

But there I was, standing in front of Sonia with this shit-eating grin on my face, my balls as soft as an old sponge, feeling like la Mollie was still rubbing her fingers slowly across the backs of my knees, and so spaced out I couldn't even laugh when Sonia finally stops yelling at me and launches into this story of her visit with her mother.

She found her mom sitting up real rigid on the living room sofa like she was a visitor in her own house. She was dressed all in black and hanging on to the biggest rosary Sonia ever saw. Her dad was nowheres to be seen.

"Mama, what's wrong? What's happened to Papa?" She thought maybe her dad had cancer or was having a little fling on the side. *La señora* Chacón just looked at her daughter with tears as big as the rosary beads rolling down her face. Like a martyr of the ages, Sonia said, her mom told her never to mention her father's name again in her presence. Aha, Sonia thought, he *is* having an affair and she was glad he wasn't dying of cancer.

Out loud, she said, "Okay, Mom, let's go to the church. You want to? You know you'll feel better if you talk to the priest." And then, Sonia told me, her mother didn't say a word, but just got up from the couch and walked straight past Sonia out the door like she'd been waiting for Sonia to ask that all along.

When they got to the church, her mother pushed her down into one of the pews and told her to wait for her. Then she turned and marched to the door of the confessional. Sonia said her mother musta thought she was walking into Father Murguia's cubicle, that old priest who's been in the parish forever and gave Sonia her first communion wafer twenty years ago. But somehow or other she got her directions crossed. Maybe her mom was confused after the whole week of going without sleep or something, is what Sonia thought. The next thing Sonia knows, her mom's fainted out into the aisle and this young guy Sonia's never seen before and who looks just barely old enough to be ordained rushes out to see what happened and, all in a flurry, they take her mother outside into the fresh air.

The priest excused himself before *la señora* Chacón came to. When she realized where she was, she stood up real dignified like nothing happened and told Sonia to please take her home cause all she wanted to do was lock herself up in a room and stay there for the rest of her life on earth. All the way to the house, Sonia kept asking what happened but all her mother would say was, "I can't talk about it, I will never talk about it." She just stood there all stiff with her fingers working her beads. "Just let me live out my days in peace with my rosary and my prayers," and off she went to her bedroom.

Well, it wasn't til late on Sunday afternoon right before

Sonia had to leave that her mother finally came out, with her face looking like a dry river bed, and told Sonia the story in such a quiet voice that Sonia could hardly hear. It seems that for the first time in their married life, Sonia's dad used a rubber. Just for the hell of it. And right after it was over, her mom knew she had committed a mortal sin cause she'd let him.

She was so embarrassed she couldn't hardly talk. Never did she have to confess such a shameful act to a priest, and she was beside herself with guilt. And when she realized she wasn't talking to Father Murguia but to the young priest, she was paralyzed. It got worse and worse. The young priest didn't understand her broken English, and when he couldn't get her to describe what exactly she did with her husband, he said "Did he want you to put his penis in your mouth? Is that what you're trying to tell me?" Well, Sonia's mom ain't never even heard of such a thing and that's when she fainted away like she'd been struck by lightning.

Sonia's laughing when she tells me all this, and about how while her mother was talking she'd cross herself every two minutes with that huge rosary and how the tears would slide down her cheeks every time she came to the parts where she had to use bad words. She said her heart ached for her but she was also having a real hard time keeping a straight face. And she's exploding telling me the story.

Catholics, man, specially old Catholic ladies are a hoot! Her mother told Sonia that her life would never be the same and she wouldn't never be able to show her face in that church again after all her years of devotion. What would people think? she kept asking Sonia. And how could she look that young priest in the face after such words passed between them? She said she just wanted to die.

But then, after her mother told the whole thing, she started relaxing a little bit. And right before Sonia left, her old lady even asked if people really do such horrible things. "Don't you think that's hilarious?" Sonia asked me twice before I answered, with a real fake smile, "Yeah, your poor old mom." I was so flipped out on my own memories that in my imagination I was halfway between Nebraska and Utah on la Mollie's body, grateful that my old man made me learn all them place names, and thinking that Sonia's mom woulda had a heart attack if she ever found out a third of the stuff la Mollie and me got into while she was getting educated in a Castroville confessional.

For a coupla months, fool that I was, I tried making it work with both Sonia and la Mollie, juggling one around the corner while the other was coming in the front door and not paying no attention to that saying that when you play with two, you end up with none. It was Sonia who broke the ice and said real direct, no bones about it, "Louie, if you're messing around regular with another woman, you gotta move out of my place. Right now." And then, like she's reading my mind, she says, "I bet you're hooked on some gringa with blonde hair and freckles. All you machos in your thirties love getting pussywhipped by white meat at least once. Why is that, Louie?"

Well, of course, I denied it and then made it worse by saying she was the only woman for me, how could she think I was even looking at someone else, specially some dried-up prune of a gringa, and so on and so on, using my hands to back up my mouth. You know, all that caca guys say when they know they're guilty but wanna keep up the show that everything is hunky-dory. You ever done that, man? And the whole time I'm talking and denying what she said, and we're swaying across the kitchen to the bed, I knew that she knew I was lying through my teeth and she was just waiting for me to make a slip so she could catch me with the goods in hand.

One night she said she was going to a party and staying over in Sausalito and some of her fairyland friends were gonna stop by and pick her up. I asked her if I could borrow her car and she said, "Sure, baby," so cool and natural I shoulda known something was up. But I was too high on la Mollie to notice nothing like that and so I went ahead with my own plans to go to this new drag queen place in the Tenderloin with la Mollie and her buddies. I ain't all that crazy about drag queens, you understand, but when I was with la Mollie, I didn't care where we were cause all I saw and felt was her.

So I wait til Sonia leaves, take a real long shower, put on my best threads, splash that Joe Namath cologne all over my body, and go for my woman in the other woman's car. I'm telling you, us guys are real dense about things like that. If I had a car and Sonia borrowed it to go see another guy, I'd kill her. How come it don't even come to me that my life is in danger? Cause I'm in love and eating cotton candy clouds.

The evening is perfect San Francisco—one of them tropical Lauren Bacall nights. Being in love throws fairy dust all over everything, even sleaze, and the scummy Tenderloin glows after a rain that leaves all the lights shiny and blinking like chorus girls. Even the porno shops look clean, and the garbage on the street's beautiful to me. I see the ugly two-bit whores walking around and they're like duchesses. I even liked the show, man. Some of them guys looked so much like women, they coulda fooled me, Louie Mendoza, expert in the art of sniffing out the real merchandise any-time, anyplace. Not even the creeps in la Mollie's party were getting on my nerves. Bruce Lugosi was all hyped cause he just made a killing in the courtroom and went so far as to pay for one round of drinks. Big fucking deal, since la Mollie and me had to pick up the tab for the rest, but even that don't bother me. I was in seventh heaven stepping out with my lady, feeling more like the prince than the toad cause la Mollie only had eyes for me. And before I could think about it, the waiters on roller skates wearing miniskirts and mus-taches were announcing last call in high falsetto. We said so long to Bruce and the rest of the bats and la Mollie and me walked—it was more like floating— to Sonia's car.

When I opened the door to let la Mollie in and then went around to the driver's side, I saw this two-tone titty pink and charcoal gray '55 Chevy make a U-turn in the middle of the street almost running down some of the people coming outta the clubs. But ol' Louie-in-love still don't suspect nothing, not even when six or seven blocks later I saw that Chevy was right behind me and didn't have no lights on.

La Mollie and me were stopped at the light on Geary and Van Ness across from Tommy's Joynt. My friend Bar-bara Dean has worked there since the dawn of time and that place won't have no existence for me when she leaves, man. I'm telling la Mollie about Barbara and the next thing I know, Sonia's knocking at the window on my side. Which like a dummy, I roll down. She sticks her head in practically half-way across the seat to get a good look at la Mollie just to make sure she ain't no drag queen and then says as sweet as chocolate kisses, "Hi, honey. Did you have a good time with your friend? I hope my car didn't give you no trouble. I know it's been acting up lately."

Sonia stops looking at me and gives la Mollie the once over so's she can be dead sure, and then she gets that smile of death that means there's gonna be all kindsa caca in the air when I get back to the Mission. La Mollie don't say nothing, just stares straight ahead like only the windshield and Tommy's Joynt exist. Then, pulling herself all the way outta the window, Sonia says, "See you at home, baby," like I'm her long-lost little boy, and struts back into that Judas Chevy, her ass swinging from side to side all the way.

Well, la Mollie kept her cool and didn't even mention nothing all the way back to her parents' place out on Seacliff Drive. She was housesitting for em while they took another trip around the world to fix their marriage and I'd been hoping she was gonna invite me in. She was chatting about this and about that, like nothing had just happened and so I thought, naturally, that I was gonna be in like Flynn, no love lost.

But women have their own rules, man, which I can't never figure out. When I park in front of her daddy's mansion, I start to get out so's I can go around and open the door for her just like a real gentleman. She puts her Vivien Leigh hand all gentle on my sleeve and says, "Don't bother, Louis," in a real cold Anglo way, the way Leila P. used to sometimes. "I can't stand two-timers. Don't call me until you've taken care of Miss Puerto Rico. Then, maybe, I'll see how I feel about seeing you again." And without a peck on the cheek or nothing, she's out the door and into Tara. Just like that!

I took my time getting back to the Mission, I can tell you, stopping for about an hour or maybe longer at the all-night donut place on 20th Street to have a cup of coffee. Donut holes—glazed or plain—go on sale by the dozen after two A.M. at this diner, and usually I can scarf down two dozen. But I was too in love to eat a donut or a hole and feeling real guilty about Sonia. Love and guilt, love and guilt, man—my all-time favorites! It seems like I can't never have one without the other. I've stopped asking why.

I love being in love. It's the biggest drug of all for me, man. All it takes is snorting one line or taking one toke of romance, and it's all over. Once you're hooked on love like me, though, withdrawal can kill you. Cocaine and marijuana, even all that alcohol all those years, ain't nothing compared to the being-in-love-every-moment-of-the-day-and-night high. It musta been all them Hollywood movies I seen when I was a kid. I believe in that stuff.

And this is where it got me. I loved Sonia and was in love with la Mollie. One made me feel guilty and the other made me feel good and my head knew that the one that made me feel good was the one I shoulda felt guilty about. I was staring at both the donut and the donut hole on the plate in front of me like they were droppings from outer space, seeing that the donut is guilt and the donut hole is love, and wondering how come I always eat the one that's gonna give me a stomach-ache?

Sonia got her revenge. When I finally got back to her place on Guerrero Street, all my clothes, my books, my sax, my music—everything including a sickly plant we called "Poochie" cause it smelled funny—was teetering on the curb out front. Naturally, the street-sweeping machine had already rolled by and sprayed the junk and dirt from the gutter all over em.

And when I walked up the front steps with my keys out and ready, there's a note taped to the front of the keyhole that said: "Drop the car key *and* the house key through the mail slot. If you come in, I'll kill you. If you take the car, I'll call the cops and tell them you stole it. I hope every *cucuy* in town gets you!" She don't need to put in that last remark, man. She signed the whole thing with a big "S" that took up half the page and then at the bottom she put a P.S. "Don't call me. I *mean* it."

The message was pretty clear, man. But the whole time I'm trying to see what I'm gonna take and what I'm gonna leave under the bushes and pick up later in my brother's car, I'm arguing with Sonia under my breath and telling her she's just another Mexican virgin martyr and a fag hag and a snake and I wished I never met her and so on and so on, the way guys do when they know they done wrong and are too chicken-shit to admit it and say they're sorry. Finally— it took me forever to sort things out cause I kept tripping into the bushes—sax in one hand and my toothbrush and comb and some underpants and a coupla shirts in the other, I'm ready to leave Sonia's life forever. Thank God she put out the sax, man, even though it coulda got stolen.

But just before I'm ready to split, I stand in front of the building and look up at her windows. I feel like she's been watching me from behind the blinds cause I see them slanted down in my direction. It's fucking four-thirty in the morning and the fog, which usually don't come down thick into the Mission, is misting over everything til the street lamps on the island in the middle of the street are starting to get real eerie like the you-know-whats. Anyways, I look up at her place for the last time and yell as loud as I can, hoping they can hear me all the way down to Army Street, "Hey, Sonia! You're the biggest *cucuy* of all!" And I run like a track star toward my brother's place in the Castro. I get away from the street lamps by turning up the first corner I come to, man, running away into the dark cause I got caught with my pants down.

Sonia and I made it up a little when I got back for the rest of my things, but she never let me in her bed again, whatever I try to make la Mollie think. Like that stuff I yelled at la Mollie when I left this morning about Sonia coming to watch me play? She don't hardly never come and see me, even at Big Eddie's. I was just hurt is all, and I can't do nothing with that kind of pain except bite back. Sonia's a sweet lady but it's only la Mollie for me, man, Grace or Marilyn or whoever she's playing.

Even telling you this story about Sonia just brings me back to la Mollie and that magic grassland over by Kezar where I saw the couple kissing away in the shadows back of the Stadium late yesterday afternoon. Kezar's like my home plate with la Mollie, man, cause it's not just where our eyes got glued to each other that first time, it's where we finally got back together. It was real romantic, the rehitching, and walking by that place always makes me all nostalgic. Cause like a knight from King Arthur's court, I had to get through lotsa obstacles to even talk to la Mollie again. Only we don't have no more dragons to con with our swords nowadays. We got phones instead.

After she stopped hanging up on me every time I called, I invited her in a real contrite, real nice John-Boy-of-the-Waltons voice to go to a football game. It was just some local high school championship but I couldn't thinka no other place where she wouldn't be expecting me to pull some crooked move. My intentions weren't too honorable, I can tell you cause you're a guy and you know what I'm talking about. I was dying to get my hands and everything else on her again. I was a driven man.

But so la Mollie would trust me, I decided we had to get together again outdoors with lotsa other people around, just like when we first met. Of course I was hoping it would all end like that first time too, but I decided I had to play the role of a happy-go-lucky guy that's never had no dirty thought in his life—one of them toothpaste-and-shaving- cream all-American dudes on TV who still look like little boys at thirty-five. Lotsa women go for them guys. It brings out the mother in em and all they wanna do is hold them anxious asps right up against their tits.

But football ain't no love-in. Later, la Mollie told me she agreed to see me cause she had this theory she wanted to prove. It was my first peek into la Mollie and her world according to theories, man. This one I call her "Kezar Theory" cause since then, no matter how hard I try to think of something else, all stadiums—even the ones that ain't shaped like bowls—make me think of one thing and one thing only. Vaginas.

I know, man, I had the same reaction. "Think about it, Louie," she said, real Doris Day, with her strawberry blonde hair shining like the moon under the stadium lights. "Just look at the shape," and she puts her thumbs and forefingers together just right. "And everything that goes on in them, especially football, is sexual."

"Oh," I say, Mr. Rock Hudson struck dumb. "That's very interesting." I'm wondering if she hasn't gone Halloween on me in them long weeks we weren't making it together. But she looks as tasty as I remember, even more than tasty, so I keep my mouth shut and give her my doctor's stare.

"And, in the case of football," la Mollie says turning into Greer Garson playing Madame Curie, "the sexuality is homosexual." Meanwhile, all them guys down on the field are beating the shit outta each other.

"Oh," I say again. Paul Muni couldn't of done no better,

man. "Please, go on," I say, examining her with my eyes. I'm thinking that maybe la Mollie is testing my manhood and wants to find out if I'm really into women—though how can she have doubts? Anyways, that kinda test is right up my alley and so I nod and look at her real clinical.

"Forget that you're watching a simple football game, Louie," she says in what I call her Official Theory Voice. "Look instead at the symbolic game being played just above the players' heads."

Well, I look, man, and I don't see nothing, but what la Mollie sees is a buncha men in tight pants bending over a ball, asses in the air, waiting for a signal so they can go after the true object of the game. And do I know what that is? she asks. By now, I'm wearing Andy Hardy's blank face without no idea for another show. "Penetration," she says, tightening her lips and making a little smacking sound with em to settle the point. I'm in gagaland, man.

"Yeah, that's right," I manage to say, but inside I'm feeling this great big laugh coming on.

"Subconsciously, these males are penetrating the other males so they can score. It's all a painful initiation into a world where women are absent, so the men have to act out the female roles. Think of our words for the players, the 'tight end' and 'wide receiver,' Louis." She called me "Louis," man, right there in the middle of Kezar Stadium, and I was so lost in the color of her eyes that I didn't even get mad and warn her never to call me that nowheres. Meantime that wide receiver has just been creamed and he's having a hard time getting up but la Mollie is in a world all her own and don't notice.

"In this case," she goes on, not even seeing the smile on my face, "the football itself is not a ball but a symbol of penetration once it is set in motion. It is the fatal agent in the destruction of male innocence acted out on a grand scale before your very eyes. And you do have such nice eyes, Louis," she says, and I stare even harder at her to keep control of the near fatal explosion inside me.

"There are more gatherings of the collective unconscious in places like this than anywhere else in the nation," la Mollie says, going back to her Theory voice. "All these people are witnessing an ancient, primordial ritual that has the same magnetic attraction that Italians find in opera, Russians in dancing, the British in the English language, the Latins in love." I like that last part, naturally. "And so you see, Louis, that's why stadiums are shaped like vaginas." The guy on the other side hears her and gives her a look she don't see cause she's facing me and is still lost in her brain.

Well, I'm lost, too. I'm too out of it to ask her if the people in the stands—like me and her—are pubic hairs or what? Later, I point out to her that if the stadium is like she says, then the guys on the field are right in the middle of it, so how can they be queers?

And she says that shows how ignorant I am about sexual theory cause everybody—later, I learned "everybody" was all them vampires in her group, including the ghoul of deprivation—everybody knows that homosexuals—she tells me not to call em queers—don't never wanna leave their mother's womb, cause they wanna identify with it. So they unconsciously yearn to be penetrated and all those guys down there are simply going through an old priapic exercise that dates back to cavemen times, or for as long as there has been a collective unconscious. The next day I looked up "priapic" in the dictionary and had to laugh at la Mollie. She has more fancy words for dick than anyone I've ever known, man.

But I point out to her that the idea of the real game is to keep the other guys from penetrating your territory. And she says that only proves her theory correct cause there is some complex called "attraction/repulsion" and everybody knows that all homosexual males are gay and miserable at the same time. Well, I can't argue with no "attraction/repulsion" theory, man, when I don't even know what it means.

Whenever la Mollie's in one of them Theory fits, whatever I say just proves what she already knows. Like this "passive/aggressive" theory la Mollie tried explaining to me one time when I wouldn't talk to her for two weeks cause I found out that her and Dracula spent the night together. Just to think of him touching her anywheres was enough to make my skin crawl off my body faster than a flea off a burning mattress.

Of course, la Mollie blamed me for it happening at all, cause she was sure I was still seeing Sonia on the side. I *was* seeing Sonia again but only like friends, like I told you, and I was using her to make la Mollie jealous, but of course it backfired on me like jealousy always does. But I wasn't gonna tell la Mollie that, so when la Mollie told me about Bruce and her, I just shut up, figuring since I always talk so much she wouldn't be expecting the silent treatment. I didn't think there was nothing passive about not talking. When Louie Mendoza don't talk to somebody, that means I'm real angry and ready to kill. For them two weeks, I played Robert Taylor to her Greta Garbo after Camille goes off with the Baron. It was one of my great performances, man, cause what I wanted to do most was have la Mollie hold me close against her Garbo skin and call me "Louis" all night long.

But once la Mollie gets an idea into her head, there's no talking or not talking her outta believing it. You just have to ride it out til she comes up with a new theory to get rid of the old one. The worst ever was when she and Dracula were into those Self-I-Zation seminars that were gonna show em all how to create and control everything. I thought I was gonna go back to the big donut and start drinking myself to death all over again when la Mollie and the parasites started with that "get it all cause you're responsible" training.

That stuff was just perfect for la Mollie and her Klan, man, cause it gave em a way to do what they want and not have to feel guilty. You ask me, they're always looking for how to manage other people. Them people like to talk about how they "share" this and "share" that, but share is the last thing they want to do. They're into *control*, man. I come from a big family, and I know what it means to have to share. Mostly, what la Mollie's gang means by share is for you to tell em a secret so they'll have something on you. I had a real hard time even talking to la Mollie then cause she could only speak in these robot words like outta some school book and every time she said one and stuck out her jaw at me in that all-knowing way, I wanted to sock her.

One time, with a smile she stole from Ali McGraw when she's dying of leukemia and looking like a *Vogue* model doing it, la Mollie tried to get me to go to a newcomers' meeting with her. What I didn't find out til later was that she and them advanced Plutonians were gonna watch us through one of them mirrors where they could see in but we couldn't see out. Ain't that the limit, man? Do you blame me for wanting to give her a knock in the head?

It mighta been diffrent if she'd offered to pay for my ticket, but she told me that part of the training was that we had to figure out a way to pay for it ourselves. "I ain't got no two hundred and fifty dollars," I told her. I knew for a fact that her rich daddy had paid for *her* and that as long as I've known her, she hasn't done an honest day or night's work, but I kept my mouth shut.

Then for about a month after I said no, she don't say nothing but just gives me them real forlorn looks, like Joan Fontaine mooning outta the windows of Manderly. She acted like I was lost in ignorance forever and couldn't never hope to be enlightened and get *It*, whatever *It* was. The next month after that, la Mollie goes to this new seminar and comes home "creating" and "uncreating" everything. One day I existed and the next day I didn't and sometimes I couldn't tell which was which or which way I'd be better off.

Finally, I told her, "Mollie, you are giving me the creeps and getting real Halloweenie on me. You're even starting to remind me of them *cucuys*. Could you please give *It* a rest for awhile and come back to us clods down here on earth? Please, Mollie."

"I am resting, darling," she said. "I have never felt more serene in all my life. You just don't get It, Louie. And at the rate you're going, I don't think you ever will."

Well, it was harder and harder to live with the It goddess, let me tell you, and I longed for them times when all she knew was funny football stuff. One night, she wanted me to stand naked in front of her and see if she could create and uncreate an erection from across the room. Nothing happened, man, cause I felt so goonie standing there with my dick just hanging between my legs like a used balloon all shriveled up. "Mollie," I said, "it won't work unless you take off your clothes or at least get that Buddha look off your face and put a little Mae West into it."

"Oh, no," she answers. "I'm not falling for that line. Just concentrate. Clear your mind of all impure thoughts."

And she makes a triangle with her hands in front of her face and just under her nose.

Well, I tried but it wasn't no good, so of course she blames me. "I can't help it," I tell her. "My dick is already there and not even I can control it one way or another when it wants or doesn't want something. Give me a chance, Mollie. I know ways we can make it go up and down. Get off that high horse and come over here."

Well, she don't go for that neither. It's too simple and natural. "Oh, Louie, you are so hopelessly earthbound. I give up," she says. And she storms outta the house like Eve Harrington on her way to take over Margo Channing's part in a play.

You know, man, I am earthbound. I don't dig people like la Mollie sometimes who want more than what they already got—which is plenty, let me tell you. When they do get more, they're still not happy and keep wanting and wanting, going around and around in a wider circle making the Nothing in the middle bigger and bigger.

La Mollie says it's cause I don't understand about ambition and power and history, even though I told her I seen *Macbeth* and look what ambition done to him. That's not my history, man, cause I come from under the bridge, like I told you, where no one wants to look or write about. But la Mollie's right if she means I don't wanna run around like her and her bloodsucker buddies in some kinda three-ring circus. I never liked circuses, all them caged animals did nothing but depress me. And all them clowns around la Mollie don't look too happy to me, man, playing little gods and trying to make the world run according to them. When she gets on that bandwagon, I end up in the middle of la Mollie's Nothing space playing the cheese stands alone and feeling like the Third World.

I gotta tell you something real interesting. While la Mollie and me were going through that creation business, I had a dream about Evelina that has stayed with me ever since, like it's part of my blood and bone marrow, man, if you know what I mean, and I think about it a lot whenever I'm in that arboretum. I don't know if dreams are what she means by creating and uncreating, but if they are, then I gotta hand it to la Mollie—we can make the world look like we want it to, sometimes anyway.

In this dream, I'm falling asleep sitting straight up on my favorite bench in the arboretum. It's a real small bench in front of a little pond and you can look beyond to a grove of trees. I'm looking across the water toward that clump of trees and there's a young gingko and a young magnolia standing side by side. Did you know that gingkos are pre-historic? I don't know about magnolias. Anyways, the strange part is that the leaves of the gingko are bright, bright yellow like they are in the fall and the magnolia is in full bloom like in late winter. I know it's a dream and that the seasons don't matter. I'm telling you cause I loved seeing them two young trees together like that.

I start saying my old man's mantra—"maple, cymbidium, lobelia, eucalyptus"—over and over before I drop off. All of a sudden, right in the middle of the dream, I'm feeling awake and watching Evelina rise straight up outta the pond with tears in her eyes and sliding down her cheeks. She walks over the water and onto the grass very, very slow towards where I'm sitting. The way she moves is how I know I'm still dreaming cause everything is so real. I wanna turn away cause I can't stand to see her crying but her face is like a magnet and I can't stop myself from looking right at it.

I feel it's autumn in the dream, my favorite time of year. People say there ain't no autumn in California, man, but there is. It's like a beautiful woman so mysterious and soft that you can barely feel her touching you, but you know you're being touched cause you got shivers like a cold, winey light sliding down your throat.

My dream was filled with that feeling and as Evelina came closer and closer, I saw she was smiling and that she was telling *me* to stop crying and get up and dance with her. And I did, and she was leading me round and round on the grass while I held to her hands, and laughing and laughing at me cause I couldn't stop crying, even while her and me were dancing.

The cackle of the seagulls fighting for something at my feet woke me up. I hate gulls, man, they're the crows of the sea, big mean bullies, ugly spirits. I can't say enough bad things about em. I yelled at em and for once, they flew away cause something in my eyes musta told em I would wring their stupid necks if they didn't split. I sat down on the bench again and tried to bring back the feeling of the dream.

I couldn't just then, but for the first time since I lost her, I said her name out loud. "Evelina. Evelina." And after I sat there for a long time, some of the feeling of her dancing and laughing started coming back to me real gentle, like a melody I'm hearing from a long time ago and don't reconnize too good, like a place I used to know but never been to. I looked down at the front of my shirt as I got up to leave and it was all wet. For a second, I thought them dumb gulls had peed on me outta revenge and then I realized what it was from and that I was still in the dream. I looked up and saw the gingko and magnolia, all yellow and soft pink, across the water.

Then I woke up from the dream inside the dream all sweaty but smiling. It's the only time I ever dreamt of Evelina and I hope it's the last, cause ghosts oughta be left alone and in peace.

CHAPTER III

That Old Black Magic

T hat's how it is with memory, man, it's sneaky like the border patrol, waiting to pull you in just when you think you're free. But even Evelina and the arboretum didn't help me forget la Mollie and that damn comet whirling around my brain. Once the spell of the trees was broken I didn't stay too long. I figured I'd start walking cross the Haight to the Castro and the gig in the Mission to make the scene early and start setting up before Big Eddie got there.

You know the Castro? It's like a twenty-four-hour Mr. World contest, man. When I got there, all them guys were flexing their pecs on their fire escapes like they were putting the make on the sun, which was setting behind them buildings. It's the saddest part of the day for me, man, when the light's starting to change from day to night and the dark's coming on like a big wet heavy wool blanket all smothering and scarier than the pillow Othello uses to snuff out his darling Desdemona. There ain't nothing nobody can do to stop the light from going to the other side of the earth and I get real low thinking about how it's gonna happen, no matter what.

Once it's finally covered you, it's okay. Most times in the desert there was stars, and once a month you could count on the moon to be almost bright as the sun. I can't figure out why, man, but it's the getting dark that gets me.

It makes me think of razor blades slicing you up without you knowing it til you look down at yourself and see nothing but blood all over.

You dig the end of the day, man? I think we're all real scared of it only we'll do anything to deny it. I call it the Caveman Hour cause that musta been when drinking began, when those prehistoric people huddled around them big fires telling each other stories to hold off the dark. It's the old drunks like me who are the most scared of all cause we're the most sensitive people on earth, though we're always pretending not to be.

You know what I'm thinking right this minute, man, is that maybe Hamlet was a drunk, only instead of Ripple rotting out his royal brain and making life a constant Caveman Hour for him, words were his drug and he used em against himself and everybody else every chance he got, which was mosta the time. God, I wonder what Leila P. woulda thought of that idea? Once, when I told her I hated Hamlet, she said it was cause I was just like him and couldn't keep my mouth shut.

To get my mind off the sun plopping into the sea, I usually look real careful at all the colors in the gardens til they fade out and the fake electric street shades start taking over. The lobelias are there to help me get through the change cause they're more neon than neon, man. The diffrent greens of all the plants send out real soothing notes into the air. You don't even have to be high on something to feel it.

The dark's just beginning to get to me when I run into my brother Tomás on his way to The Neon Chicken for dinner with some of his buddies you know are gay cause they're all trying to look real tough in their leather and cowboy outfits. One of em is an offensive lineman for the Raiders, man,

I ain't telling you which one. But the dead giveaway is that they all got these perfect haircuts and their faces are so clean they look like daisies all fresh and ready for plucking.

It's none of my business what Tomás does with his dick, man. He's my brother. My business is to love him, right? But it's hard to keep my mouth shut about his life sometimes. Like last week when I stopped by to see how he was doing, he and his buddies was talking about some big-time San Francisco lawyer who was into bondage and wound up smothered by these heavy chains wrapped around his chest. Whoever did that to him left him hanging in a leather sling with two bottles of poppers up his nose. The guy's ribs had caved in cause of the weight of the chains and poked his lungs fulla holes. One of my brother's leatherette friends wondered if the dude had done it to himself, sorta like the gay Jap writer they're all reading. I can't thinka his name, but you know the one I mean. He committed Harry Carey *and* had his head cut off cause nothing was perfect enough for him. I'm telling you, man, these sissies have a hard life. I'm serious.

I keep quiet in them discussions cause I don't wanna say nothing to insult Tomás or make him think I reject him. But all the time they're talking about the dude in the sling, I'm thinking that maybe he's better off dead steada in the kinda hell that got him into that sling in the first place. But I don't say boo. Once my brother seen I wasn't gonna put him down or nothing for being what he is, Tomás and me were okay except for the older brother complex he says I have about him. "Stop taking care of me," he tells me, but I can't help it cause I know most everybody around wants to kill guys like him. I know I went through a time when I felt that way too.

When I was thirteen and a coupla brothers in the gang

and me were jerking off in old lady Pompa's basement landing—she was deaf and blind so nothing woulda happened to us even if she had opened her door and caught us— Mosca Villanueva stopped for a stroke or two and said, "Hey, ain't this what queers do?" And Oscar Manda answered right in the middle of hitting the bull's eye we had painted on the wall four feet away, "No, man, the queers love each other."

The way he said it taught me a lesson right then and there that's stayed with me ever since. In this world, you can't love guys and jerk off with em at the same time cause if you do, you're queer. But when I look at Tomás, I don't see no fag. I just see my brother, so I worry about him, cause the world has a helluva lot more Oscar Mandas than Louie Mendozas.

I walk with Tomás and his gang to the front of The Neon Chicken before I head off for the club. Tomás tells me they might stop by later and catch a few numbers and I say, "Okay, *carnal,* but don't kiss me in front of Big Eddie. He don't like it." Without skipping a beat, he says he won't, that he'll just grope me and plant a sloppy wet one on Big Eddie. I give him a hug and start walking down 18th Street towards Mission.

On the way, I try not to pay no attention to the way the guys walking up to Castro Street keep looking first at my crotch and then at my face the way straight dudes look at girls' asses and legs behind their backs. I don't understand guys making it with other guys but as long as they don't mess with me that way, they're okay, man. It's mostly the straight dudes who go around raping people. They're the ones I'm scared of when I see em coming towards me in a pack.

It was Virgil Spears taught me about queers, man, I ain't ashamed to tell you. He was the first guy to ever beat me up. His dad was a drunk and his mom split long before Virgil even got to grade school. He and his dad lived right on the edge of the barrio in some one-story apartment building that was always being condemned. It was only a coupla blocks from where me and my family lived in the projects. We ran into each other on the street when we were both fifteen and right away I said that only fags were named Virgil and he said, "Yep, that's right, podner," and let me have it, a left hook to the jaw that had me reeling for days. Naturally, in a week, we were shooting pool and having beers in some Juárez dives where I knew none of the gang would run into us. They wouldn't of liked me hanging around with a sissy.

Virgil told me that his mom left cause she couldn't take his dad's drinking no more, and left him behind cause she didn't have no money and was only nineteen and heading back to her parents in North Dakota. She promised to come back for him as soon as she could, but he never saw or heard from her again.

In the meantime, his Jack Daniels ex-Marine poppa did all kindsa things to make a man outta him and make sure he wasn't no momma's boy on his way to being queer. Like he'd throw him into pools before he could swim and not let no one help him out til the last second. That went on the whole summer Virgil was four til the lifeguards complained to the Recreation Department and little Virgil and his daddy weren't allowed into no pool in the city limits of El Paso. "That decision probably kept me from getting polio in the epidemics—you remember em, Louie? And by the end, I was learning to relax and float. Not bad for a little pansy, huh?" He made like he was gonna punch me and I ducked, man. He had a mean left.

But the worst was the year his old man decided he was gonna teach him not to be sentimental. Virgil told me this story about six months after we started going across the river on a regular basis. "Crying's for girls and homos," his dad kept telling him. "You're going to be a man even if it kills you, boy. We're not training any fruits in this outfit." So every month when Virgil was about seven, his dad went to the pound and got three or four puppies he said he was gonna give away to friends so's they wouldn't suspect nothing. He made Virgil feed and take care of em for a coupla weeks. Then, by the dawn's early light of the last Sunday of every month, he punched Virgil awake with his boot and said, "Okay, boy, let's go to Sunday School."

He made Virgil ride in the back seat with the puppies and drove em out to the desert along the Carlsbad Highway. They'd park on some dirt road and head to a lonely ravine where he made Virgil stand at attention while he shot the puppies one by one. The first coupla times it happened Virgil closed his eyes and cried or tried to put his fingers in his ears but his old man got mad and ordered him to keep his eyes open and dry and his hands down by his sides or else he'd use a Bowie knife and do it real slow.

Virgil was scared his dad was gonna kill him, so he did what he was told. Finally, after about eight of these executions, he phoned the pound and told em what his daddy was doing and the Sunday slaughtering stopped. Virgil got sent to a foster home for five years and then sent back to his old man on a trial basis when his daddy promised to sober up and keep his son in school and away from trouble.

"Did he do it?" I asked him.

"Well, I'm with you, ain't I, podner?" and gave me a cowboy whoopee.

By then I was having a real hard time keeping my eyes dry thinking about that little kid out in the desert with nobody to help him out. La Pixie woulda cut that crazy Marine's balls off and served em up to him in *albondiga* soup if she had known what was happening just a coupla blocks away from her. She couldn't stand no stories—real or made up—about kids or animals getting hurt. When I told her about the concentration camps, she cried and prayed for a week and said them children that died should be made into saints even if they was Jewish. "Don't forget," she said to anyone who argued against her idea, "Jesus was a Jew," and the discussion was closed.

Virgil told me his dad kept trying to treat him bad again but by then he was getting big enough to fight him off and the old guy left him pretty much alone. "He figured he'd done what he set out to do." At the moment, Virgil was setting up a three-ball combination shot. "Once he saw I was strong enough to kill him if I wanted to, he made up his mind I was finally a man." He got all three balls in and I watched the cue ball roll real slow to just behind the eight ball inches from the corner pocket. Man, that gay boy could sure play pool.

After I thought about it for awhile, I brought it up one time that maybe all that stuff that happened when he was a kid was why he decided to be queer. We were right in the middle of another night of pool and beer in downtown Juárez. Virgil laughed for awhile and kept beating me every game as usual, but faster. He kept looking at me funny like he was sizing me up and didn't know if I was gonna be able to pass or not. Finally, he said, "Louie, you big crybaby, look at me and tell me exactly when you decided to be straight. I wanna know the moment you looked down at your crotch and your brain told your dick it was only gonna be interested in pussy for the rest of its life. Come on, Louie. Tell me. And don't lie, Aztec man. Tell yourself the truth for once."

Well, I thought about it and before I could come up with something to break the silence, he says, "You see. You can't tell me. And you know why, bean breath? Cause it's not something you decide with your head. Hell, if that was how it worked, I'd decide to be straight in a second. You sons-of-bitches have the whole world at your fucking feet and nobody minds you screwing as long as you keep away from the real little girls. It's just a damn sight easier all the way around." He sipped from his beer bottle and looked at me funny one more time. "But it don't work that way, tortilla face, no matter how many priests or Bible-toters you got telling you it does. And Lordy-Lordy, those dudes are scared silly of the sex inside themselves and they're gonna make damn sure everybody else is, too. You listening to what I'm saying, taco ears?"

Even though he was talking low and smiling I could tell he was angry. I remember that he walked over to the table and picked up the cue stick real serious, then set it back down and came back to where I was standing at the bar. He wasn't finished with the lecture and before I could say I was sorry I even brought it up, he gave me a look that read every sexy thought I ever had and said, "My mommy and daddy didn't turn me into a queer. It's there right from the beginning. I'm a natural born fag just like every other fag I've ever known, even the ones that go around saying they're AC/DC. Gay or straight's not something you decide with your brain. You ain't dumb, Louie, though you act like it. Think about it. You got more than beans for brains. When you can tell me the moment of the day or night you chose to be straight with your head, I wanna hear about it. You show me that moment and I'll follow you to the promised land of pussy."

Well, I still don't have no clue about that moment, even now. I just know that I can't have sex without pussy and that's how it is for me. Back then, all I could say to Virgil was something lame like, "Well, what did you learn from your old man and how come you're still calling the old fucker 'daddy'?"

And just like he knew I was gonna ask him that, he says, "I learned never to be like him if I could help it and how to sleep real late on the last Sunday morning of every goddamned month. And I call him 'daddy' cause that keeps him human. If I didn't, then he'd turn into a monster and I would end up killing him and me too."

He bought the beer for the rest of that night by way of thanking me, he said, for being somebody named Louie Mendoza who listened to a queer named Virgil. I even let him hug me—in a friendly way, of course, I don't want you to get any ideas about me that ain't true. Almost a year later, when his old man shot himself—pointed his shotgun right at the roof of his mouth and pulled both triggers, man— I went to the funeral with Virgil and stayed with him at his place, day and night, for a week. I didn't even care what any of the brothers in the gang thought about it and they don't say nothing to me.

He spent the first coupla nights with his head on my shoulder or in my lap, crying and crying all them tears he never cried for his old man, asking me over and over how come the fucker didn't just let people love him. What was so goddamned hard about that? I told him I didn't know.

77

Even me, Louie Mendoza, the great people reader, had no answers for him.

There ain't supposed to be no Anglo fags in Texas, you understand. Just real heavy dudes and rangers that ride their horses and Harleys all the time, fuck their women good, and drink everybody under the table if there's one handy cause usually they're out on the range shooting deer and hunting down Mexican aliens. God, Texas is the strangest state of mind I can think of, man, and the only thing I miss about it is the southwest desert where the stars really are big and bright and have nothing to do with what goes on deep in the heart of— clap, clap, clap-clap. I always hated that song.

But that Virgil Spears, he was just a big cowboy, the only guy with a Texas accent I could ever enjoy listening to. He had his own way with words, and he taught me that all fruits and sissies aren't no Nancy Marys and weak little mothers. I'll never forget Virgil—he left El Chuco the end of our senior year and took a Greyhound to New York City—cause he laid one tall story to rest for me, man.

Thinking about Virgil, with the dark coming in all around, made me sadder than I'd been all day and I started wondering if maybe la Mollie was right about that stupid comet. I was on Dolores Street then and I looked up at the sky but couldn't see nothing cause of the fog. The city was on its way to becoming a Cloud Cuckooland and if the world was gonna end, it was gonna do it without no witnesses.

Dolores is my favorite part of the Mission. I love to walk down them islands of palm trees they got planted in between the lanes. Did you know that palms were brought in from the deserts on the other side of the world? I like to think these come from Egypt. I'm crazy about how them big spidery fronds wave at me and I respect *them* more than the quaint Spanish Missions everyone gets ga-ga about. When I look at those white adobe buildings, all I can think of are all the Indians who got whipped and killed putting em up just so some Spanish monk could lord it over em all humble-like and superior and get made a saint for doing it.

And then they gotta go and name this whole part of the city after them church buildings like the priests oughta get credit for the Chicanos who're trying to make something of themselves when they don't care caca for no one. You probably don't know the Mission too good, man, but it's getting bad down there. The kids start smoking weed and fucking before they're ten years old. They're mostly Mexican and Latin American so nobody at City Hall or in them churches does much to help em out. They get real mean to get attention.

The only thing worth looking at in the Mission Dolores is that giant bougainvillea that covers one whole side of it and blooms practically half the year. But it's them palms that are the oldest real creatures on Dolores Street. They just give out their strength and power without no sermon or wanting something in return. All trees are like that, man, their arms forever open to the world. I wouldn't wanna live on no planet without em. Even in the winter when some of em lose their leaves, they're still standing there, all calm and ready and offering you something good.

When you cut over from Dolores near the corner of Nineteenth and Valencia, there's the Busy Bee Market, where I used to hang out when I lived with Sonia just a coupla blocks away. There's a real friendly feeling around the Busy Bee cause the swinging doors ain't automatic so people are always closing and opening em up on each other, which gets them talking. And there's this redhead checker named Joyce O'Leary I used to flirt with. She's in there like always when I come by, ringing up groceries and bagging away. I catch her eye and she gives me a big Irish wink. She's talking a blue streak to some neighborhood wino I know is asking her for credit. I also know Joyce will give it to him and then pay whatever it is herself, but not before he has to listen to her lecture on the evils of drink. Specially the kinda shit he's pouring down his throat.

"If you're going to drink, Walter, drink the best," Joyce is telling him, her Irish accent in full gear and all her "rrr's" sounding like they're related to bears with burrs all over em. "Have the courtesy to listen to Sister Joyce, and greet the Lord with Black Label on your breath, not this putrid seventy-four-cent piss in a bottle." All the time she's talking, she's bagging away and humming some good witch tune.

Joyce is one them good witches, man. She used to be a nun til she got wise and decided that before she could be a saint, she had to live with the poor people, not only pray for em. "Just like dear sweet Jesus on the Cross," she used to tell me when I'd stop by and go on coffee breaks with her.

She limps, wears wire-rimmed glasses, and she's only got one eye. On the lens that covers the missing eyeball she paints diffrent colored, very real-looking eyes every week. The color depends on her moods. When I first met her, I didn't know which eye to look at.

Joyce talks more than anyone I ever met, even me. I know you don't believe me but it's true. You oughta record her, man. She got this definitely working-class accent and I never heard no one play with English like her. It's like she wants to destroy it and have all the fun in the world doing it.

I fell in love with her "r's" and wanted to teach her how to roll em the Mexican way but she ignored all my signals and went right on talking about how she had to save enough money every month to keep her daughter in some fancy Catholic girls' school. Then one day, this ex-nun says as casual as if she was offering me half a donut, "You want to do it with me, Louie? We could have a rip-roaring, red-hot time," rolling her "r's" the Mexican way. I pretended she was putting me on cause I'd already turned her into Ingrid Bergman playing Joan of Arc *and* that Sister from St. Mary's both at once. So Joyce starts laughing cause I ain't no good at hiding what I feel when I'm caught off-guard. She tells me not to worry about it, that she knows I have a girlfriend.

Later, when I was sleeping on my brother's couch and breathing fairy dust without no Sonia or la Mollie, I tried to take Joyce up on the offer but she just gave me a Judy Holliday look outta her plumbago blue eye, the real one, and instead got me to talk to her about Evelina and my old life—the bad part—without me even noticing she was getting more outta me than me outta her. When I told her I was moving outta the Mission, she gave me a kiss on the cheek and said goodbye like she'd been saying it all her life to everything and everybody. The Irish and the Mexicans, man, they understand life the same way.

I tried to call la Mollie on the phone outside the market but the line was busy, and then when I tried again she don't answer even though I let it ring and ring for at least twenty-five times, which I count so's I can tell her later when she scolds me for not calling her. This means she's playing Blanche DuBois all delicate and fragile soaking her creamy body in a Vitabath and thinking how all guys are nothing but brutes.

At least I hope that's what she's doing and not getting herself ready to go out for a night of bloodsucking with Mr.

Know-It-All. I don't let myself think about that or I'll go wacko bananas. But I gotta give up on talking to her before the gig, I figure, and instead scoot my ass on down to Big Eddie's all set to knock em dead with my sax.

There was still a little light left in the sky but I see that the neon outside the club is already blazing away, which surprises me cause Big Eddie's such a tightwad he usually don't turn stuff on til it's completely dark. The whores are walking up and down the street in crotch-length miniskirts, their tits playing peekaboo with the dudes driving by in their limos and giving em the once over. Them guys bother me more than the fruits, man, cause they think money can buy em anything and they treat love like a business, which it ain't. Love is love. At least the fairies have some romance going for em. I never met more romantic people than them. My brother and his friends are always talking about "the perfect relationship" or "the biggest dick" or "the buns of death"—idealists, every one of em. That's how come women hire em to do their living rooms or their hair. They know them Tinkerbells are perfectionists. Can you imagine the world without em?

But these dildos on fancy wheels, everything is too easy for em. It's still early so there ain't too many around yet, but before I run upstairs into the club, I flip one dude the bird and describe something his mother is doing to half the Forty-Niners football team. Mr. Slick is too stunned to answer back.

The minute I'm in the door and up the stairs, the air feels so heavy I know that Big Eddie is already there. Sure enough, he's sitting at the bar not looking one way or another, but straight back at himself in the big mirror. Big Eddie's one of them old-style machos, man, the kind that has to feel he's in charge of everything or else he turns nasty—

Marlon Brando doing the Godfather for laughs without meaning to. He looks like a Mexican Viking with a clipped dirty white beard and a full head of hair cut real short like a monk's and dark brown eyes set in cream jelly cause he drinks too much. When people treat him like royalty, Big Eddie talks in real short sentences through gritted teeth that are all yellowish-brown. He thinks that's the way real men are supposed to talk but I think it's cause he's got a simple mind.

Big Eddie walks around with this cane he lets everybody know has got a pure gold handle. He swears it helps him keep his balance. He don't hardly ever lean on it, though, but uses it more to slam doors shut or turn light switches on and off. He let the story get around that he was wounded by shrapnel fire in World War II. His leg looks okay to me, man, and his hands are real soft. When you ask him what happened, he gets all teary-eyed and self-pitiful and says it's too hard for him to even talk about it. Then he'll let it drop that he was in the Pacific "keeping them midget Japs from landing on America's sacred shores," and next thing he'll say is that he got wounded on D-day while he was on his way "to personally teach that little Kraut with the moustache what a real American was all about." I think he's been watching too many movie re-runs on TV, man, but I don't worry about it cause I'm pretty good at handling his kind. I been around em all my life.

I learned a long time ago not to mess with other people's idols. It don't get you nowheres, and idols crumble all by themselves. But it gets me how many people worship Big Eddie to death, specially the women. You'd think they'd see right through the guy. Instead, most of em cry when he makes his war speeches or sit there with big eyes and their panties getting all wet when he tells em about all them bull-fights he seen in Mexico. I gotta admit that when I first heard him, I thought he was a pretty great talker, too. He could shine a big spotlight on some pretty dark things. But after awhile, it was like he was doing imitations of himself. When he ain't running his jazz joint, he goes up to Napa to have breakdowns.

Big Eddie's one of them Chicanos that moved away from the Texas border towns to East L.A. in the twenties and thirties, and he's got this real big chip on his shoulder about the ones who stayed behind. "They ain't nothing but servants, man, doomed to failure," he told me in this real confidential tone when he found out I'm from El Paso. "There ain't no real Chicanos in Texas no more," he says. "They even hate the word. But before I die, California is gonna be a Chicano state. Wait and see." Maybe, but we're still gonna be poor and the lawyers will figure out a way to keep us in the working class and the teachers will still be arguing about what way we got a right to talk. But I don't say none of that, man, cause I know better than to make a peep when Big Eddie is doing his cosmic predictions straight outta the pages of *Time* magazine.

When we are all playing our parts right, we fool Big Eddie into thinking we're his slaves, and he gets real generous and there ain't nothing in the world he won't do for us and the band. Or at least say that he'll do. But if any little thing goes wrong or he imagines that someone is not showing him the respect he wants, look out, man, cause Big Eddie turns into Citizen Kane raging for a lollipop someone stole offa him!

When la Mollie first met him, she took one look at the way Big Eddie was walking over to the table with that cane swinging in his delicate hand and said so's only I could hear, "Oh my God, he's just like my father." I thought I was in for some fireworks, but then the whole time he sat and talked at us, butter wouldn't melt in la Mollie's mouth. Big Eddie was having a time calling her "honey" and "sweetheart"— which she hates and won't never let me do it—and staring at her legs, touching her every chance he got. La Mollie's batting her eyelashes at him like some Barbie doll on diet pills and tossing her hair around in more directions than I got on *my* compass anyways, talking to him in a sweet baby girl's voice all fulla sugar for her Big, Big Daddy. It was sickening and the two of em kept it up for three and a half cocktails—which they let me pay for—before Big Eddie pulled in his horns and excused himself so's he could go take care of some business. The way he got up from the table made his business sound real important and delivered the message real clear to la Mollie that it was more important than sitting around in her company anymore.

"What a creep," she said before he was too far away and I ain't sure if he heard. If he did, he kept right on walking. "A real snakeface," la Mollie goes on, her eyes all hard and flashing. "He's the kind who thinks foreplay is a snap of the fingers before he sits on your face." La Mollie has a real dirty mouth sometimes, man, specially when she thinks the world ain't treating her like it's supposed to. I know enough not to say nothing or complain that she ordered the most expensive drinks in the place believing he'd pay for em. She didn't know no better.

Later that night, when Big Eddie met me coming outta the john, he says, "That sure is some ball breaker you got there, Louie. She's gonna eat you alive, spit out your heart and stomp on the pieces. Don't expect me to come to no rescue. She's the kind that wins Miss America contests and turns into the Snow Queen when there ain't enough cash around. You better watch out for yourself with that no-good gringa gal. I know what I'm telling you, Louie. What happened to you and Sonia, anyway?" Shit, man, la Mollie and Big Eddie are two of a kind and don't even know it.

Maybe we're all like that a little, you know, hating the people we're like. You ever do that, man, get these bad vibes from someone and not know why til all of a sudden you think about them and know it ain't really them that's bothering you? And like sometimes they can be people who seem as far away from you as Mars? You ever feel that with guys like me, where you sit down to study em under your microscope and you find yourself looking in the mirror or wondering if they use the same kinda toothpaste?

Boy, I sure have, lots of times. Anyway, la Mollie ain't come back to Big Eddie's since that night and I ain't heard a kind word from either about the other one, so the best I can do is just keep them two as far apart as I can.

When Big Eddie catches me looking at him in the mirror, his face turns Orson Welles and I know what kinda night it's gonna be, though I didn't know the half of it yet.

"Hey, Big Guy, whatsa matter?" I ask him like Paul Newman talking to George C. Scott in front of a pool table. I love Newman, man, I wanna be him when I grow up.

"None of your business," Big Eddie says like a spoiled baby and orders a double shot of whiskey. I can tell he's already had a few and I figure right away it must be woman trouble cause I don't see none anywheres. I ask Jimmy the one-hundred-and-nine-year-old bartender for a soda water with lime. Big Eddie keeps him around cause he don't have to pay him union wages. Never mind that Jimmy can't hardly tell bourbon from gin any more. He lost his sense of smell after the third fire that almost destroyed the joint. We knew it was Big Eddie's way to get more insurance money for something he had to have, whatever it was.

When Jimmy brings me the soda with lime, Big Eddie says, "What are you? A fairy? Have a beer. One beer ain't gonna hurt you. I'm worried about you, Louie," he says looking at me in the mirror looking at him. "Your get up and go has got up and went."

"I don't drink when I play," I say like it's no big deal and change the subject by asking him about his mother. Bingo! She lives with him or he lives with her, I ain't figured it out, but I got the right question. And cause it's just him and me, Big Eddie tells me about it in big long sentences that wind like spaghetti around a fork.

"I don't know what I'm gonna do with that woman, Louie," he says. "She's driving me to an early meeting with St. Peter. All day she's screaming and hollering at me cause she can't find this wooden spoon she's used to make spaghetti sauce ever since Jesus walked the earth and that's been in her family since before Adam and Eve and if she don't find it she'll never be able to make spaghetti again the way it's supposed to be made and is it my plan to get rid of her in pieces like this by taking one precious thing after another away from her til there's nothing left? And on and on she goes, until I have to leave the house I paid for with my balls or throw her outta the window which even wouldn't kill her but would cause me to have to take care of her invalid self and listen to her every wish for the rest of my rabid life on this planet." All that in one breath, man, no lie! Real soap opera. He woulda made a great Chicano tenor, better than Pavarotti.

Then, a little calmer with a touch of tears in his voice,

he says, "All I have ever wanted, Louie, believe me, is a little peace and quiet, that's all, and now some fucking wooden spoon, for Chrissakes, comes between me and the little I have ever asked for outta life. Help me, Louie. I'm gonna die." This is the real Eddie, man, the one he ain't about to let any woman see.

I just let him keep talking into his booze. What can I tell him? With Big Eddie, you learn to listen cause if you try to help, it's never good enough and just adds to his misery and he'll be sure to let you know how much.

And while he's talking about his mother and then about women in general and how they ruin the lives of every guy in the cosmos, I see Tito walk in with his drums and I give him the signal to come over and rescue me from drowning in a plateful of pasta. The rest of us in the band just want to get outta Big Eddie's way, specially when he's into his suffering. But Big Eddie loves Tito and always pays attention to him. "Hey, Eddie," Tito says. "How they hanging, Big Guy?" Tito's real nice and toady and I know things'll quiet down, so I excuse myself and go to the john.

On the way, I try la Mollie again cause how long can even Blanche take a bath? And when she don't answer, I start getting a queasy feeling that I think now was telling me that she was right about the comet after all and that something terrible was gonna happen. But just like a guy, I don't pay attention. I'm looking in the bathroom mirror and watching the cold water run down my face, thinking that there's a *cucuy* hiding in one of the stalls and just waiting to get out and hound me for being so mean to la Mollie and walking out on her the way I did. That's what I thought then anyway. Now I'm not sure whether that *cucuy* wasn't trying to warn me about what was coming instead of blaming me for what already been. I left the john real quick without bothering to dry my face, I'm so anxious. I shoulda just kept walking all the way outta the joint and back to la Mollie to be there when the comet hit. But no, I'm a man, I can take anything and don't have to believe in nothing.

At the bar, Tito has done his job so good that Big Eddie agrees to pay us in cash right after the gig—not in food or in drugs or by check, but in cash, man. That's a real big concession from Mr. *Chingón*. "What did you promise him, Tito?" I ask. "A blow job?"

Tito laughs and says, "Yeah, man. He can do me anytime he wants." He starts setting up his drums, the instruments of doom for the night, you'll see why.

The other guys are tuning up and Big Mamow, our keyboard lady, has for once showed up early and is picking out a tune that she knows I dig. Big Mamow's a farm girl from Nebraska who moved to San Francisco during the summer of love. She ain't married and the guy she thinks is the father of her fourteen-month-old kid was some junkie AWOL from the Navy, so she hasn't seen him since she found out about his habit too late to have an abortion. Then a month before she had the kid, Big Mamow ended up right here in this dump of an ER heaving in hell cause of some bad chicken enchiladas with sour cream she calls her gringa enchiladas.

When I brought her in here to get em to stop up her guts, I thought she was gonna lose the baby right then. Them doctors did all right by Big Mamow that night. But a few months later when she brought the baby into the clinic upstairs for a checkup, the stupid intern told her that the kid had cerebral palsy and would probably never walk. I thought Big Mamow was gonna have a stroke.

"She was this little terrorist, Louie, who laid this whole trip on me and then sent me and the baby to Physical Therapy where I had to wait another four and a half hours for two more flunkies to argue with each other about whether or not that first lady was right. Now I don't know what to believe or think except how I'm going to kill myself and that child too if she's got that disease. I can't even say its fucking name it scares me so much."

I kept trying to tell her she wasn't gonna kill nobody, except maybe that intern, and that the baby was gonna be just fine. She leaned a little to one side, that's all. Five months later I watched that kid take her first steps and she's been tearing around Big Mamow's house in Glen Park ever since. She's my goddaughter so of course she's already talking a mile a minute and every time I ask her for a kiss, she closes her eyes—she's got these big lashes that musta come from her father—and Frenches me. No lie. Women get started on making life right from the cradle, man. Her name is Emma.

Sometimes I wanna murder every doctor I run into—like now, for instance. What the hell is taking em so long in there? Is this normal, do you know? I know la Mollie's gonna live cause she came to in the car and didn't stop talking til we got here even though she was still bleeding like a stuck pig. They're probably scaring her into a coma.

"How's the baby?" I asked Big Mamow just as we're about to start the first set of the night.

"She's in Big Eddie's office, sleeping." Big Mamow fluffs up her thick dirty blonde hair and turns into Marlene for about five seconds. "With the spaghetti spoon. Big Eddie gave it to her last week to keep her quiet." And she laughs this big wheatfield laugh that's all her own. Me and her have had some good times, man, and the best of em are when she's on keyboard and we're trading the melody back and forth til we come up with something in between that me and her never imagined.

The crowd don't start coming in til after the first set, which was too bad, cause I did this great ad lib in my solo for *Kansas City*. I love that song, man. It makes me wanna move to anywheres where there are pretty women and forget everything bad that ever happened. It's one of them forever tunes. Every forever song has its own special color, and when I'm really into it I turn that shade. *Kansas City* is real bright orange, so when we're playing our rock 'n' roll version I become a giant navel orange blowing a tenor sax— wearing sunglasses, naturally—all juicy and ready to explode and splatter myself all over anyone who's near me.

Only about a dozen people besides Jimmy and his assistant at the bar heard me. And Big Eddie, of course, though he was pretending not to pay no attention, but I could tell he really was cause his cane kept thumping in time to the music. He was happy again cause he'd found the spoon and the customers were starting to come through the door in bigger and bigger parties.

I don't never know how my ad libs are gonna go, man. That's part of the fun. It's like a diffrent spirit takes over and I just follow it down a road. Sometimes it's paved with diamonds and sometimes it's only gravel and dust. I was on my way to Emerald City that night and *Kansas City* was my ruby slipper. That's the way it is sometimes, man, when you play your best stuff and no one's around to hear it or if there is, they don't know what you're doing anyways. I've learned to play for me. And for Big Mamow and the guys too, naturally, cause they know what I'm saying.

By the 11:30 set, though, the joint is packed and pepper hot—about seventy-five people and not just the sleazos from the neighborhood. Some Pacific Heights matrons all wearing their Gucci, Pucci, Halston, and Saks tinkle in with these young hunks on their arms like they just got outta the Opera House to do some down and dirty slumming with the natives. A jolly green giant is with em, rounder and a little shorter than Big Eddie, and he keeps winking over in my direction like he knows me or wants to. Every time he laughs, he makes everybody else he's with break up just cause of the way it sounds. I musta met him when la Mollie took me to the opera that time, but I couldn't figure it out.

Anyways, I wink back not thinking nothing about it and now I'm glad I did, cause maybe I brought a little excitement into his last hours. At a table across the room from him is a group of leather and chains guys, some of em only half-dressed so's everyone can take a look at their washboard stomach muscles. Their black leather caps are still on their heads and they have handcuffs and other stuff hanging from their belt loops to the right and left. I forget what my brother told me all that meant but it has something to do with Top and Bottom, all that either/or shit. They look pretty tame to me and they're celebrating someone's birthday and buying drinks for all the people on their side of the room. Girls from off the street come clicking in and out with diffrent guys or with each other cause they like the music. It's your basic San Francisco crowd, all mellow as Jello, out for a friendly good time and trusting that all the strangers in the room'll peak at the same time on whatever drug they're on. Big Mamow, the guys and me go into our salsa version of *That Old Black Magic* just about then to help em along.

That's another of those forever tunes, man, only it's about lust and I know that monster, let me tell you. The more you feed it, the more it wants til there ain't no more to give. And then your mind takes over and starts lying to you and whispering in your ear and saying that you do have more and the next thing you know you're out on the streets when where you should be is at home in bed alone reading the comics, cause only laughing can break the spell. You don't believe me? Don't judge til you've lived it, man.

One time la Mollie and me went to this porno festival in North Beach and the audience was put into that deadly quiet lustland by some chick on the screen who's blowing thirty guys into paradise in exactly thirty minutes. That's her claim to fame, man—Donna, Dominatrix Without Mercy, guaranteed to make em lose it in less than sixty seconds—and we're all sitting there in the clutches of the lust monster along with Donna. Then she looks directly at the camera with a big yummy-scummy smile on her all-American face and asks in a real pouty way, "What am I going to do now?" and some chick from the audience yells out, "You're going to brush your teeth, honey!" Well, we laughed our asses off and the lust monster right outta the theater.

The way Big Mamow, Tito and me arrange our version of *Black Magic* is so that we make people feel the power of lust but not to the out-of-control point—almost, but not all the way out. Lust is a dark oily color with all the hues of the rainbow so's it looks black. Me, I become a boa constrictor playing this tune, curling and sliding along a branch above the dancers' heads, ready to drop on em when they least suspect it.

We start out soft and almost slow, bolero style, and as we begin to get into it, we pick up the pace a little, just enough to be noticed by them parts of your soul that lust likes to prowl around in, and then we get louder and louder but still keep the same holding-back salsa beat while each player has his say. Then, right when it seems like all the elephants and whales in the world are shrieking in heat and making it with each other in and out of the jungles and the oceans and we've got sirens going off in all the dancers' heads, but all just a little bit slow, we bring the whole thing down with a sigh and shudder here and there from Big Mamow's keyboard, Tito's snare drums and my sax, just to let everyone know, in case they didn't feel the boa around their necks, that we've given em the best musical orgasm of their entire lives on the planet.

This time, though, when we get to the elephants and the whales, everybody's drug seems to be kicking in and the place is going wild. Big Eddie is waving his ignorant cane in the air to keep some people from dancing on the tables and the bar. The Pacific Heights dames have let their hair down and are all over the leather men. One of the muscle guys has stripped down to a studded black leather jock strap, a coupla the girls from the street are topless, and even the opera dames have taken off a layer or two. San Francisco never lets you down, man.

To help everybody ease up a little, we slipped right into another kinda forever tune—*Body and Soul.* Me and the room are turning into this far-out purple color and everybody's dancing real close with everybody, they don't care who. We're right in the middle of the song when the world falls apart. I'm on my way to becoming a Satsuma plum from Santa Rosa when I see this guy in a weird suit walking through the crowd straight towards me. I wouldn't of noticed him except for the suit and the way he's slicing through the dancers with a real dumb look on his face like he has to go to the bathroom or bust a gut.

Then, about five feet from the platform and right under the rim of my sax, he stops in front of this couple who're dancing like two vines that came outta the same seed they're so twisted round each other. He pulls out a piece, grabs the guy's hair and yanks his head from the broad's chest where it's been resting. Then he shoots him, twice, right between the eyes, like they do in them spaghetti westerns. That part is all slow motion, man, like when you're in a car and you're watching another car that's gonna hit you and everything gets unreal, like the whole thing is happening to someone else and you can't stop it, however long it seems to take. Later, you realize it all happened in a split second and you start shaking like a desert squirrel lost in Antarctica. I hate it when time does that, man. It ain't natural—that slow, slow part, then everything all loony-tunes like a chase scene in a silent movie.

That's the part that hits me now, right after the slowmo bangs. The girls and the guys start screaming. I look over towards Big Mamow but I can't see her nowheres. The killer is running back out through the crowd, but with all the loony shuffling he can't get through and he starts firing some more. Then the whole place goes Keystone Cops and I see the jolly green giant fall over backwards in his chair. One of the jock strap guys gets it in the leg and starts yelling louder than the girls. Then one of them bullets musta hit Tito's drum, man, cause it starts making this pinging, hissing sound I'll never forget, like the air was going outta the world. That slowed everything a little and brought me back down to earth and into real life.

This is gangland, man, heavy drug country, where any kid high on PCP could go crazy with or without a gun, and I'm starting to panic thinking what if we're all in the middle of a neighborhood war? Big Eddie or somebody else stupid turns out the lights about then which makes everything worse, and I can hear Tito yelling for us to get the sweet Jesus outta the joint before we all get killed.

I'm yelling for Big Mamow but I can't hear no answer. The lights are blinking on and off, on and off, like we're inside a gigantic strobe, and people are going around in circles looking for the exits. No one's doing nothing about the guy lying on the floor with blood coming outta the two holes in his head. Big Eddie, of course, has locked the front doors so the cops can't get in and bust him for not having no dance license. Turns out he's refused to pay off the cops on the beat that week cause he didn't like the way one of em looked at him.

Me and Tito somehow end up scrambling to the back stairs before anybody else finds em and I'm almost two-thirds of the way down when I make the mistake of turning around and looking up. Tito's still at the top trying to carry all his drums so he can't see nothing. Tito is not one of your brighter guys but I never realized how really dense he is til last night, man. Weed will rot your brain every time.

All of a sudden, Big Mamow is right behind him holding Emma real close and screaming, "For God's sake, Tito, leave the fucking drums and get outta the way!" And like the dumb, mariwacko jerk that he is, he drops em all and they come crashing down straight towards where I'm standing. Most of the deadly mothers roll and bounce right by, but the second-to-last one crashes into my leg and hits my shin so hard it seems like I can feel the cracks creeping out and up and down and around the bone, and I'm watching it shatter and crumble in on itself like in a cartoon. I thought I was gonna die. I hung on to the banister to keep from passing out from the pain.

Let me tell you, man, I ain't never felt that kinda pain before, not even in Korea when I smashed my thumb with a hammer in twenty-below weather. Tito's down the stairs by now picking up his fucking drums. He grabs me and starts shoving me towards that cockaroach car of his saying, "I'm sorry, I'm sorry, I thought she was a ghost!" and I'm screaming for him to let me alone, not knowing what fucking ghost he's talking about.

"Big Mamow," he yells, "I thought the guy shot her, too."

I start shouting at Big Mamow to get herself and Emma the hell outta there before the cops come and Tito's dragging me after him along with them drums I never wanna see again, which he throws in the back seat, breaking one of the windows. That's gonna cause trouble later, you'll see, but right then it didn't seem to matter cause the car looks like it has the plague anyways.

While I'm leaning there against Tito's car I see Big Mamow with Emma in her arms disappear around the corner and into the night. I'm feeling the pain shoot up and down through me like grass on fire and Tito's pushing me into the car and trying to get both my legs inside the front seat which, naturally, is all the way up to the dashboard cause Tito's old lady Santina has the legs of an elf and likes to pretend she's a headlight when Tito and her get high on weed. I'm shouting at Tito to undo the seat lever, cause it's always stuck and he's the only one who knows how to do it. But when he finally gets it loose, the seat slides back so fast, my left leg that the drum has mangled for life, the one in the cast here you're gonna get to be the first to sign after we're done with this talking, it hits the gear shift and I faint. That old black magic has cast its spell, man, in reverse.

The next thing I know, Tito's pulling up in front of this

godforsaken hospital for my first visit of the night. It's early morning and you're like sleeping in your bed somewheres, right? While I'm opening my eyes and seeing nothing but the flaking ceiling of Tito's car and I'm thinking that life after death is not what I thought it might be.

"Am I dead?" I ask.

"No," Tito answers from far, far away. "It's your leg."

"My leg is dead?" I'm not yet conscious, man. "God, Tito, are you stoned already? What are you telling me?" By then, I'm starting to catch on and don't even wanna look down cause I know I'll see this knobby branch that used to be my leg twitching like a busted worm on the floor of that VW bug, totally separated from the rest of me. It's one of them awful moments in life, man.

Pretty soon, cause I'm flashing in and out through the pain that's screaming at me, I catch on that Tito's trying to pull me through the car door cause he wants me to walk—all by myself—into the emergency room. He's scared his drums and the weed he has in the glove compartment will get stolen outta the broken window in the back, he tells me. I look at him like he's crazy.

"Jesus, Tito! You want me to die right out here on the street? It's your damn fault the drum smashed my leg. I don't give a shit about it or your stinking weed. Let the fuckers get stolen. Help me, man." But reason don't get nowheres when it's talking to a stone, man.

"I'm sorry," Tito says again. "I really did think she was a ghost." Then, one more time in case I missed it, he adds, "I ain't leaving this car by itself around here."

For about twenty seconds I wanna be Godzilla and grind his Bambi face into the steering wheel. He musta noticed my look, cause he starts honking til an orderly comes out, sees what's going on, and pries me outta that VW without bothering to ask me where I'm hurting.

Ever notice how nine times outta ten, the people who work in hospitals don't seem to understand poor people in pain but don't have no trouble with the rich? Seems like everything they do to help you—how they touch you or move you or talk to you or look at you—just makes you hurt more. They even act like it's all your fault that you are sick or hurt or fucking bleeding to death. This orderly was one of them nine so insteada letting me lean my right side against him, he keeps knocking my mangled leg up against his all the way in here. But before he gets me outta the car, I make Tito promise on the soul of his long-dead grandmother, who brought him up cause his mom got run over by a trolley on Market Street during a heavy rainstorm, that he will wait for me, no matter how long it takes.

"Hey, don't worry, man," he says under his breath. "I'll just roll me a doobie and lay back. I can use the rest after all the excitement, huh?" I can tell he really don't register how hurt I am.

"You promise to wait for me, Tito? You promise?" I'm practically begging by then, too much in pain to act like anybody but me.

"I promise," he says, like he means it, and gives me that goofy smile that shoulda told me I couldn't trust him to be there when I got outta that inferno.

The orderly leaves me sitting for fifteen minutes of eternity til this cute woman typist who looks like Minnie Mouse and reminds me of my cousin Patti asks me to walk across the room, sit down in the chair next to her adorable little desk, and answer a few questions. I tell her I can't walk—that *that's* what's bothering me—but she just looks at me with them mouse ears and eyes like she don't see the blood running down my leg or hear what I just told her. In a funny mouse way, like she's four-legged, she walks across the room to her desk, sits down, and just stares at me, changing from Minnie into one of them Pod People from *Invasion of the Body Snatchers,* man. I can tell she's gonna sit there til I do what she says or die. So I hop over and fall sideways—left side, naturally—into the chair and almost pass out again but I'm too scared to do that cause I don't wanna end up in Pod Land with her. I force my eyelids to stay open for the half-hour that she's asking me all them questions about insurance and what drugs I've been on and am allergic to and what do I do for a living and can I do the samba and every goddamn thing they ask you while they watch you make like the Invisible Man from loss of blood.

The whole time she's handing me these forms that I gotta sign without really knowing what I'm doing or get thrown into the dumpsters out in the alley along with the rest of the body parts. By the time she's done all I wanna do is throw up, and I'm wondering how I'm gonna keep my cool in fronta all the other people waiting around for help. We all look like we're in the cast for *The Night of the Living Dead,* man. You're lucky to be here now cause this place is even creepier at night when there's no light coming in from outside and them fluorescent things make everybody look embalmed.

Last night, or I guess I should say real early this morning, when the world is supposed to end and I'm starting to believe it's gonna, right over there in that corner by the other desk there's a drag queen dancing around—more like making little jumps—with an electric wire hanging outta his dress. He's in as much pain as me and he keeps trying to

100

get the nurse-in-charge to pay attention to him. She's busy doing something else, God knows what, and keeps telling him to sit down and wait his turn.

"But you don't understand, you don't understand," the guy says over and over again. "I can't sit down until I get it out. Please, please, please, please, please help me." I gotta feel sorry for the guy, you know, even though I'm starting to get the hang of what his problem is and my own leg's throbbing with every beat of my heart. I have to go to the john, naturally, but I don't dare ask where it is, and I sit there and try to think of something besides my bladder. At least the drag queen is providing some distraction from my floating kidneys.

After awhile, he starts moving in these funny little Munchkin leaps that make his wig tilt backwards. With the mascara running down his sweaty face, he looks like Loretta Young playing a clown in drag. Finally, completely desperate, the guy stops jumping up and down, walks real calm to the outlet right next to the nurses' station, plugs in the cord hanging down from his dress, and starts screaming bloody murder like Norman Bates was knifing him in the shower. The nurse comes over right away, unplugs him, and takes him outta the room. I gotta hand it to the dude—he got the attention he needed, which is more than I was getting just sitting there and taking it like a man drowning in my own piss. The rest of us are staring at each other, wondering how we're gonna top that act.

It takes the doctor a coupla hours of bumping and thumping to decide where exactly my leg's broken, even though I'm pointing right to the spot and telling him exactly where it hurts the most. Naturally he ignores me til the X-rays prove me right. This dude is named Dr. Norman and he don't seem to have no clue that there's anyone else alive but him. God, I hope he's gone home by now cause I don't want him nowheres near la Mollie. He looks Jewish and Irish at the same time, a bantamweight with a little pot belly and real curly darkish-brown hair above a narrow forehead that sticks out over his beady little rat-brown eyes. The hair kept throwing me off cause it was like an Afro wig gone wrong.

He talked more than me, man, I gotta tell you, and what really got me was how he kept talking about himself like he was someone else—like he wasn't Dr. Norman but some other dude. When he first started talking that way, I kept waiting for this Dr. Norman to walk into the room. Slowly, I caught on that *he* was Dr. Norman. And he's bragging about everything he's done to deserve the attention of the whole world. Like when he first came in and seen me wincing with pain, he said, "You've got to be a man, boy. Like Dr. Norman, tough and together." Then he's off on some lecture about traumatized limbs and the extraordinary diagnostic equipment Dr. Norman has developed and has at his disposal for obtaining like ultra-precise information about these fucking bone aberrations or whatever which let him with like startling exactitude make these readjustments to produce some kinda perfect realignment that's gonna allow me to waltz again like Fred Astaire and give Dr. Norman the Nobel Prize in Medicine or something. What he was really trying to do was tell me I didn't hurt someplace and then when I kept saying I did hurt, he went back to the spot and squeezed it to make sure. A wooden boot woulda been less painful, man.

If it wasn't for what them X-rays showed, he probably woulda put a cast on my arm, cause he really wasn't interested in where I hurt at all. He was much more into where he was hurt, specially by the women in his life. By this time, the aide has given me some Demerol to keep me quiet and all I wanna do is pass out from boredom. The aide, who looked sorta human and was supposed to be helping him hold me down, would wink at me and flash these secret warm smiles to tell me to be patient and just let him talk. He walked out talking, man, like I wasn't even there. I never seen no one so wrapped up in his own little world.

After about a year of him and a half-hour of waiting after they put this cast on, the aide comes by and tells me it's all right for me to go home.

"Were you at Big Eddie's tonight?" she asks.

"Yeah, how come?" By then, I'm too tired to even wonder why she wants to know. It's the first time anybody's mentioned it.

"No reason," she says, with this funny look on her face like she knows something terrible that I don't. "A lot happened there tonight," is all she lets outta the bag, like I don't know that already. Then, looking at me like she wants to memorize my face, she asks me if I have a ride home. "If you do, you can go," she says. "The medication should be just about worn off by now. But if not, you can lie down in one of the smaller waiting rooms until someone comes for you."

Well, like the dummy that I am cause I believe the promises people make, I'm thinking that Tito is still sitting there in the night waiting for me. "No, thanks," I tell her. "I got a ride." And I drag my two hundred pound leg outta there.

Now I'm figuring that aide musta been the one la Mollie talked to sometime that night while my leg was getting mummified and she weren't no more human than Dr. Norman, just quieter. Cause the rest of this I don't know about for hours and hours til I'm driving la Mollie over here myself, but this is where the real trouble gets going, man, the one the *cucuy* in the john musta wanted to laugh at me or warn me about.

Near as I can figure, la Mollie turned on the TV about one o'clock in the morning. She made it a rule never to watch TV after midnight cause if you do, she says, you'll turn into one of them negative space aliens. That was okay with me, man. I'd rather be doing something else after midnight, or any time.

But she can't sleep, she tells me later, so TV it is, and one of them news bulletins comes on. You know, the kind that interrupt regular programs like they do to make you think the missiles from Russia are on the way and everybody on earth's got only thirty more seconds. Of course, la Mollie thinks it's gonna be about the comet. She's been waiting all day for some smart-aleck newscaster to at least mention it since to her, anyways, it's life and death stuff. But no. All they say is that two guys have been shot to death at Big Eddie's and that no names can be released pending—I hate that word, man—notification of relatives.

So naturally la Mollie starts calling every hospital in town. When she finally gets through to S.F. General, some aide down here tells her that yes, someone that fit la Mollie's description of me had been admitted earlier that evening and that yes, two guys *are* dead, but that no, she's not at liberty to give out any names. Even when la Mollie drops her family name like a bomb on the aide, the dame just hangs up on her.

You get what I'm saying here, man? The aide didn't lie to la Mollie or nothing but she didn't tell her the truth neither. She told her all this stuff but didn't tell her caca. Why do people do that, man, talk like machines? You gotta say what you know people gotta hear, man, or what we got mouths for? To give the chick some credit, maybe she thought la Mollie was the ride waiting for me out there.

But she didn't know la Mollie, man. You give her a option between happy and sad, and she'll go for doom every time. She was brought up on Romeo and Juliet, man, not by way of Leila P. like me but in the neighborhoods of *West Side Story*. The only time I feel like crying in that story—it don't matter which version—is when Juliet meets Romeo for the first time cause you know the whole thing's gonna end real bad for both of em, specially her.

So naturally, la Mollie decides I'm a goner and gets hysterical. She don't like to be treated like everybody else. She was born with that silver spoon between her teeth and she's gonna find out what happened to me, no matter what.

So she decides to drive down here herself to see what the hell's going on. But she can't get her millionaire's car started and floods the engine. Then she realizes she's locked herself outta the house, so she breaks a window to get back in again and trips off the burglar alarm. By the time she manages to shut that off, she's just tears, man, and don't know what to do. La Mollie's like that when things ain't going right for her, like a little girl who's so angry cause she can't get some clothes or something on her doll that she pulls the doll's arm off and then starts wailing about that. She's banging around throwing things and yelling my name, then she heads for the kitchen, she tells me, pours herself a vodka, no ice, to calm down and finally thinks to call Tito's old lady Santina.

Talking to Santina's like reading in the dark, man. In this marijuana haze, Santina tells la Mollie that Tito's just called her from the County Courthouse to let her know that he left me in Emergency, Big Mamow was a ghost, and he's being booked for possession of narcotics and indecent exposure. I'm telling you, man, my friends belong in a zoo.

So then, la Mollie says, she knows for sure I'm dead and thinks Big Mamow's with me on the boat to Purgatory. She hangs up and starts wondering what's gonna happen to little Emma and what's gonna happen to her. And it's then she musta realized what I been telling her from before we ever started living together, man—that she can't live without me the way a baby can't live without its mother. It takes her thinking I'm dead to finally admit it.

So, feeling like a big baby, bottle of vodka in hand—that Russian shit that's two-hundred-plus proof—la Mollie crawls back into bed and drinks and cries herself into a stupor. "I never felt so lonely and so helpless in my whole life, Louie," she tells me just as I'm delivering her to this room of doom a coupla hours ago. And I believe her, man, cause I know what vodka does to your soul. Wine is to forget and Scotch is for when you're mad at the world. Beer is for courage when you're afraid. But vodka, man. Vodka is for lay-down-and-die grief.

Of course, I don't know none of this til about seven A.M. this morning, cause at about four I'm right outside them automatic doors, standing in the fog and trying to learn how to walk again, and not sure if la Mollie's at home and not out somewhere with Dracula's fangs making two holes in her neck. I don't even remember where I left my sax and I only got a coupla coins in my pants which are all torn to shreds—the way you're seeing em now—and whatever they gave me for the pain has definitely worn off. My head is doing a slow spin towards the whirlies, and the parked cars look like dark wet marshmallows in the early morning fog. I'm trying hard to get my eyes to focus on something familiar—like Tito's dirty little cockaroach. Naturally, it's nowheres in sight, or maybe it turned into that big rat I see oozing down the gutter drain on Potrero Street.

All I could think of was how much I wanted to be lying next to la Mollie so I could tell her I would never, ever again doubt her word about nothing mystical. If we got married, she could even put that into the wedding vows if she wanted.

That's a big concession for me, man, cause I think we're supposed to take care of business on earth with the little sense we got. Calling on God or another world is for last resorts. God's got other things to do and ain't got no memory, and earth's the place to keep time. Our job is to tune into whatever's got more power than us, which is most things— the wind in the eucalyptus trees, or nasturtiums that pop up outta the ground and bust out into colors. You know what I'm telling you? Do you? Tell me the truth, man. Does any of what I'm saying make sense? La Mollie always looks at me like I'm on my way to the nuthouse when I talk this way to her.

I was cold standing there outside the hospital and getting the where-I-gonna-go, what-I-gonna-do-now? blues. So I looked at my feet—they're the most humble parta the body, man—and started putting the one in the shoe out a little ways and dragging this other one in the cast along for company. One in front of the other. It's like they're about two miles from my head. I make sure I don't look at the sky cause I don't wanna see no comet up there, man, with or without no tail.

CHAPTER IV

Avocado

The rest of last night was like one of them foreign flicks la Mollie and Bela like so much, man, all fuzzy at the edges and just a buncha little cutouts of scenes here and there that you figure go together but you ain't got a clue how. I'm standing in the fog in front of them double doors not believing that Tito's not out there waiting for me and knowing that I shoulda figured he'd be gone all along, and not wanting to go back into this neon jungle cause there ain't no help for me here neither. It's ghoul time, when Dr. Jekyll turns into Mr. Hyde and him and the Wolfman are out prowling the streets for blood. I'm howling myself, man, cause that little dose of Demerol is long gone. I wanna squeeze the juice outta Tito for leaving me alone like this, specially after it was him and his damn drums that put me here in the first place. But most of all I wanna get to la Mollie before that comet hits for real so at least we can go out in each other's arms, but I ain't sure I can drag myself down the block, let alone across town. So I'm thinking where the hell is the bus stop while I'm pulling this anchor along like Paul Muni on the chain gang and imagining all kinds of torture for Tito.

Where Tito was I didn't find out til I got back here with la Mollie a coupla hours ago. When they took her away bleeding behind them curtains and left me alone bouncing off these slime green walls, I musta called everybody I know to keep myself from going loco. When I didn't get no answers, I started thinking I was making all this up and la Mollie was right and I really *was* dead and sitting in some waiting room for the undocumented down in Hell. I even called Sonia, man, to tell her about la Mollie—like she'd care. But all I got was empty rings there too. Finally, the third time I tried Big Mamow she said hello and it was like coming back to earth in one of them gas balloons, all slow and soft and smooth.

But even though Big Mamow'd been out to Santina's and all, she was just guessing about what happened exactly, so I can't tell you for sure. Cause Santina's like Big Eddie, man, one of those people that expects the rest of us to clean up their messes. But she's all her own, too—this bird that got stuck with skin and is always trying to fly off into the wild blue or something. She's got these real tiny arms and legs with this kinda wide head that makes me think of a mushroom. She says that when she's stoned—and when ain't she?—she can remember all her past lives, but she ain't so hot hanging onto the one she's in right now. I don't know where Santina goes when she's not here, man, maybe she really is in some other life, but I know for sure she's nowhere I been or wanna spend much time soon. She's like la Mollie that way, man, using them old sins to explain how come they're screwing up now, down here in *terra firma*.

They live in worlds of their own, man. Most times I think Santina's so loony she don't know how to butter bread. But once she almost had me believing in her mambo-jambo when she was reading my Tarot cards and said I was gonna have a confrontation with an attorney who was linked up with a red-haired woman. Well, three days later, there's strawberry blonde la Mollie floating into my life like that

110

red balloon done for the little boy in that French film, man, and within a week I'm arguing with all her lawyer pals, specially Mr. Lugosi.

Still, it's hard to trust them past lives people to give you the time of day about anything that's going on down here on earth. Cause nothing ain't what it seems to them, when to me it's enough just banging against the caca this life leaves around to trip you up, let alone carrying around some dictatorship of the spirit world you have to keep watching out for. I got enough ghosts as it is, man, without needing a buncha leftovers from someone I mighta been but never knowed.

But Big Mamow's got her ways of getting down to things even when Santina is laced into her spacesuit and off in orbit. Near as she can figure it, while I was getting plastered from toes to knee by that scumbag doctor, Tito was sitting in his bug rolling a joint. For Tito, rolling a joint's a real production number like midnight Mass at the Vatican. He's leaning over that ledge of a dashboard in his cockaroach car with everything spread out all over when he looks in the rear-view mirror and sees a cop pull up real slow right behind him. You ever think about how cops got this way of showing up just when you don't need them, man, and when you ain't doing nothing to hurt no one but you're breaking some law anyhow? So there he was, with just enough dope on him to go to jail for awhile cause he's already done time for possession.

What Big Mamow and I figure is Tito went into this panic, not putting the dope away or nothing but just wanting to get outta there as inconspicuous as he can. So he musta started a real slow crawl towards 22nd and Guerrero to catch the new freeway to Daly City and disappear into the night. His idea, we decided, was to leave his drums, my sax, and the dope at Santina's and then turn right around and come back for me. Least I hope that was what he planned, man, giving him the benefit.

Naturally, the stupid bug broke down just when he got on the freeway. Least that's what he told Santina, or what she told Big Mamow anyways. What Santina kept repeating, Big Mamow told me, was that Tito got picked up right in front of Big Mamow's house, like she shoulda seen it. Big Mamow thinks she meant that it happened on the freeway, cause Big Mamow lives near enough to the entrance over there to make someone like Santina who don't know where she put her teeth sometimes think that. But the real joke far as I can see is why they got him at all. It's cause when the cops trolled by to see about the stalled car, they find Tito with his pecker out pissing along the side of the road, maybe thinking that then they'll just cruise on by. But I guess they musta slowed down or something and made like to stop and give the bug some attention, and he turned and started waving them on, still peeing away like he's some fountain. And that's it—he's busted for exposure and dope and I'm left stranded in my cast. Oh, José, can you see!

Once I told Big Mamow no one got hurt at Big Eddie's except the green giant and that dude who got it for sticking that lady—double-dealing will get you one way or another, like I was saying before—she got all apologetic for not calling up la Mollie. "I was so freaked out, Louie, I couldn't think of anything but the baby." I can't hold no grudge against a lady like her, who only wants to do for the little she got. If we were all like that more these hospital dumping grounds would be less crowded. She really was sorry, man, and worried about la Mollie and Tito and Santina and all. So I told her it was okay, that she had done good just to get outta there with Emma and that it weren't her fault but Big Eddie's, who could drop dead for all I cared about him and that toilet bowl of a nightclub of his. "People coulda been killed who weren't even there," I told her, thinking of la Mollie when I said that, of course. God, man, what if she dies?

Big Mamow was wanting to set things right, which is her way. "I'm going to go by Big Eddie's place right now and try to get him to at least lend me bail money for Tito. I've got ways to shake some of the fat off that old tub. Wish I could shake it off me!" When Big Mamow needs dough bad, she lets that *chingón* put the moves on her. "He don't do nothing but touch me where he never thought I'd let him, Louie. His hands'll grope around for a coupla seconds and then he'll give me the money I need to pay off the hospital or the rent or whatever. What do I care what he wants to turn it into for himself or his buddies? It's just a feel. Guys like Big Eddie are so scared to death of women they can't get it up anyway. Don't you know that yet?"

Well, I didn't know I knew, but right when she said that it was like instant flashbulbs and I knew I'd known that all along. Know what I mean? Funny how it happens that way sometimes, ain't it, that not knowing what you already know until someone makes you see what's been staring you in the face all along? But I didn't wanna think about Big Eddie's sex life then. I was too worried about la Mollie to care what that fucker did with his dick.

"You want me to come for you and Mollie?" Big Mamow asked me.

I told her no, and about how we had la Mollie's car and all the comet stuff and how la Mollie thought I was a goner. "You and me, Big Mamow, were so dead in her mind she figured the world really was gonna get its bell rung before the cock could crow again."

Big Mamow laughed but she didn't wanna talk no more cause she had to get to Big Eddie's. I didn't wanna let her go, I was so scared and not wanting to be alone, but I could tell she was out the door already. I love Big Mamow, man, she's a no-bullshit friend, just right there to take your hand when you can't find nowhere safe for it to go.

So near as I can figure, that's how come there weren't no Tito waiting with a bouquet when I trotted out onto the street last night. But all I knew when I left this mausoleum with my plaster pants was that he weren't nowhere in this life that'd do me no good. Instead, I'm hobbling down Potrero towards Market in a San Francisco mist that meets up with the sweat inside my torn clothes and makes me feel like I'm being dunked in cold, oily water every time I pull this leg suitcase of mine along the sidewalk. I hate that clammy feeling, man.

A coupla cars drove slowly by like they was checking me out. One of em was fulla guys and their chicks from the neighborhood who start pitching empty beer cans at my legs and one of the dudes yells out, his face all PCP red, "Hey, fag! How come you limpin', fag?" One of the girls screams, "Cause he just got laid!" and they all crack up with these druggy laughs like they're applying to work for Doc Frankenstein. I don't pay too much attention to em cause I know they won't bother me if I just act like I'm deaf. But when I take a quick side look at how many of em there are—just in case—I see the gleam of a chain with a big fake gold cross around the neck of one of the dudes. Christian chic, man, the worst kinda hypocrisy. I never been happier than when they turned on 14th Street and left me quiet to just worry about myself.

Angel dust and religion! What a combo! Them kids spend ten years getting taught by the nuns and going to Mass and not eating a piece of toast without blessing it first and all they got left is them pretty crosses. Don't even let me get started on the Catholic Church, man. When I was a kid and me and my brothers and sister went to Sunday Masses at Our Lady of the Angels we used to sit there and wonder if the priests even knew where they were. They preached at us in that pure Castilian Spanish of theirs that no one could understand, swallowing every word and lisping through these sermons that lasted an eternity or what seemed like forever, specially in the summers cause the air conditioners didn't work and them priests didn't think us dumb Mexican Indians needed no air anyways. It never failed that some poor old lady or dumb-ass kid would faint and conk themselves bad on the bench in front of them or in the aisle on them hard stone floors while them priests from Castile just went right on chanting like nothing was happening.

Whatever we couldn't understand, what them priests made crystal clear was that us parishioners needed to give more money to Holy Mother the Church and her diligent servants of Christ on this earth. Now, Our Lady of the Angels was a real, real poor parish with mostly older Mexican people that couldn't afford to leave no dollar a week in the baskets. Poor old Deogracias Rodríguez and Moises Archuleta—the two of em totaled up to almost two hundred years, man—they were the basket bearers and moved so slow, it took em the whole Mass to finish the two collections. It was a lot for me to leave the weekly quarter my dad gave me and I only let it drop into the basket in them times when I'd been real bad and confession wasn't good enough to cover my shame. God, I hated confession. I couldn't take no comfort in it like Sonia's mom used to. It always reminded me of walking into my casket and trying out eternity. I can't stay cooped up for long before I start clawing the walls.

By the time I was nine or ten, I was getting real tired of hearing that me and my brothers and sister were nothing but vile miserable sinners and that our only hope for salvation—that's another of them control words I can't stand, man, cause it's scared too many people I love into eating caca—was to devote ourselves body and soul to them, God's representatives. When I was an altar boy for them guys, sailing down the aisle in my white silks like one of them swans that drift around in the Park, I began to see that in their Spanish eyes, we were Indians, man, or worse, cause Mexicans are a mixture of Indian and Spanish. They made me feel real lonely all the time I was around em. I mean *lonely,* man. Like stranded between El Paso and Alamogordo, right in the middle of White Sands where they tested the A-bombs and missiles, far away from any road or sign pointing the way out.

So, one Sunday morning, when one of em was telling us—his voice going like a locomotive with a lisp—that if we didn't contribute more money to the parish funds, Our Lady of the Angels was gonna fold and we'd all perish in a state of mortal sin dry and unforgiving as the sun that beat down on us every day in the desert, I got up and walked down the middle aisle—all dressed up in my altar boy drag, man—real slow, so's he could see my back good all the way. I didn't worry that Father Lisp would stop the sermon and ask me where I was going. I was just proving his point about people like me anyways.

I left the cassock and the surplice under the holy water bowl at the entrance of the doomed church. And with my quarter still safe in my pocket, I walked across the street to Mr. Cursio's snow cone stand and bought me a rainbow-round-the-world special. I figured the Hell I was going to couldn't be no worse or last no longer than them sermons where I learned lots about fear and guilt and not too much about love.

I was ready for love then, real hungry for it—just a kid ready to pop like a pimple cause the girls were starting to smell so good to me. Better than those confessional screens anyway, man. There wasn't no doubt in my mind about which was holier. I was ready for my first real blessing.

Blessings and curses, man, blessings and curses and a lotta sitting around and getting ready in between. You ever think that's what life's all about? Either you're off to Oz like Dorothy in them ruby slippers and the Wizard's looking to shake hands, or you're mopping up for the Wicked Witch and wondering why you left home in the first place. Know what I mean? Like yesterday. I woke up next to la Mollie feeling like one of them astronauts bouncing around in the moon dust, with every inch of my skin exploding like the Fourth of July and ready to go off and shower the world in color. Then there I am less than twenty-four hours later, out on Potrero pushing my way through this sand dune of fog and hurting so much that I'm ready to just sink into the gutter and let the street sweepers clean me up.

A coupla other cars slid past me real slow but I didn't dare ask for no ride. I know what's driving around at that hour south of Market and I don't wanna think about em or what can happen to me or I'll never make it back to la Mollie. All I got to protect me from my own mind is my pain and it's giving me plenty to think about, let me tell you.

Over the years, I've learned that sometimes if you really pay attention to the exact spot where it hurts, you can get the pain to keep still. Maybe not go away or be snake silent, but at least quiet down. I was having a real hard time doing that cause there was lots in my head, like where's my sax? what's la Mollie doing? what's happened to Tito? did Big Mamow and Emma get home okay?—all them tomorrow things. So the steady burn up and down my leg was taking over the rest of me and by the time I got to 11th Street, I was ready to keel over. I ducked into an alley and tried to concentrate my good energy on the pain. Real deep breathing kept me from the dry heaves cause my stomach was as empty as the Chihuahua desert.

Pain ain't like guilt, man. You can do business with guilt, put it off and put it off or feed it a coupla crumbs a day just to make yourself feel good and keep it at a distance for a long time. No way with pain. It don't just sit on your shoulder like guilt. It yells and you better pay attention or else.

So there I am, all doubled up in some alley south of Market trying to zero in on the pain like a kamikaze pilot on a mission, when I spot my brother's car a coupla yards away. What the hell was he doing in this part of town at that hour, I wondered? What was anybody doing there, including me, Louie Mendoza?

I'm starting to notice there are guys in leather and Levi's walking up and down the alley and paying a lotta attention to each other. In the middle of the side street, I see about twenty-five motorcycles lined up outside some place that's hidden away. I guess the guys heading that way figure me for a drunk crouching in a doorway, so they don't pay me no mind. They're buzz, buzz, buzzing with each other like bees getting close to the hive. I figure maybe Tomás is in there and I'm starting to think that soon as the pain lets up some—and it's starting to—I'll limp-buzz over there myself and see if I can find him so's he can give me a ride and get me outta this nightmare and back to the sunshine of my life.

But nothing's that easy, least not for Bigfoot Louie Mendoza. I start to move, but the pain ain't nowhere finished with me and it shoots right through and up to my groin and gut. I get as far as Tomás' car and lean against it for dear life. I'm looking to see if it's maybe unlocked so's I could at least lie down for a minute outta the street. Naturally it ain't, and I'm stuck standing there like Edward G. Robinson facing the end of Little Caesar in front of that billboard. I know by now that I ain't gonna get control of this pain just by waiting it out or by concentrating on it cause I ain't got enough brain left to count to ten. But I got a couple more pain-killing moves up my sleeve, one of which is to start thinking about the people in my life who went through more pain than me. I'm trying to breathe real deep each time when another memory sneaks up from behind and starts its stranglehold.

I always get real teary with this one, man, I can't help it. Seems like I'm telling you that a lot tonight, ain't I, about crying all the time I'm remembering things. I've thought about that crying stuff a lot, cause if the gang ever saw me cry they woulda teased me into the next century. But I ain't no sissy, you can tell that. And the tears, seems to me, they're like the desert rains that clean everything up and make the air smell like itself again. I don't let many people see me do it, of course, but I was alone there in the alley so I could let it all hang out— except anything about Evelina, which I had to keep erasing cause thinking about her is too much to take anytime and just makes me wanna blow up like one of them James Bond cars.

So what comes to me first is a picture of these dudes I knew at the V.A. Hospital down the peninsula after I got shipped outta Korea and back to the States for going bonkers when my buddy Juan de la Torre got blown up. Me and Juan thought we were lucky, man, cause we were part of the trip-wire forces along the 38th parallel there in Korea and nobody expected much action cause the really hot place was starting to be Vietnam. We were just supposed to do this maintenance police work but that meant we was bored and on alert at the same time. It was the not knowing when something, anything, was gonna happen that got on my nerves. And then I seen Juan blown into a million pieces by accident cause the crate of grenades he was loading onto a truck blew up and scattered him to the four winds. Instant cremation, man. That did it to my head once and for all, and the curtain came down over my eyes.

After that I couldn't pretend anymore not to be bored and I couldn't pretend not to be scared. Them grenades was made in America, man, and I seen that mosta the guys over there were Mexicans or blacks and all the heroes had split to wherever they go after the world reconnizes em and pins a lotta medals on em and sticks their name in some history book. And there was my buddy Juan all over Korea, I don't know where exactly. I started shaking all the time and getting nosebleeds that made me think I was the Red Sea.

They gave me this physical but the only thing the doctor asked me was if I slept with the window open. I told him it depended. He told me to open it if I slept with it shut and to close it if I slept with it open.

"That's it?" I asked him.

"For now," he said and put some checkmarks on my chart.

The next time it happened the doctor asked me if I picked my nose. I told him I did sometimes.

"Oh," he said.

A coupla nosebleeds and two whole days of shaking later, some other doctor decided I had malaria. Then when they couldn't find no bug, they came to the conclusion that I was just plain wacko. I coulda told em that from the start, man. So I got sent back to the States where I was supposed to be shipped to El Chuco for some outpatient something. But the Army being what it is, I wound up at this V.A. Hospital to recover and didn't get back to Teresa and Evelina for another six months.

For about half my time there I was real loony-tunes cause that trip-wire had tripped my switches toward haywire. They were moving patients all around then and my group was the last of what the powers-that-be called the "non-hopeless" to be mixed up with the ones they labeled "hopeless." I couldn't tell the diffrence then, man. I was too out of it to care.

Mr. Johnson, this King Kong Swede they kept in maximum security mosta the time, was definitely one of the hopeless. You know, man, hope is a real scary thing. Most everybody always thinks it's so great and it really ain't. I think it's the other side of the coin to guilt. Hope looks forwards stead of backwards, but both of em are staring into darkness. Just like Mr. Johnson.

I never did find out his first name, cause we only got called by our last names in the Educational Therapy classes they made us take every morning except Saturdays and Sundays, when they gave our jello brains a rest. Mr. Johnson came to them E.T. classes twice a week only and always attached to a big black momma aide in her thirties who looked like a fullback for the Green Bay Packers. They was connected by a two-foot chain that started at her wrist and ended in a metal ring that was part of the harness Mr. Johnson had to wear. It wasn't no straitjacket cause his hands were free but it looked like one and probably felt worse than that to him.

Mr. Johnson was huge and never opened his mouth except once that I know about. He sat there them two hours of E.T.—even in a chair he looked six foot high—with his eyes all watery and drool oozing outta the corners of his mouth. He was so tranqued out, the aide had to wipe his face for him every five minutes. She did it real automatic but with a kinda tender movement that got my heart going again.

I can still see that poor E.T. teacher—his name was Mr. Angel, man, and he told us he was a graduate student trying to get through Stanford. The Kid had a gimp leg and a shoe with a mile-high heel. He was all ears, this real skinny guy with radar dishes at the sides of his head that picked up on everything. And he had these real delicate hands with long crooked fingers. I can still see em writing things on the board real fast like they had a minda their own. Every time he called my name during the roll call—and he said my name right cause he told me he was from El Paso too—I raised my hand and said, smiling like the idiot they all thought I was, "He's not here." I said it with a real thick Mexican accent, spraying "h's" all over everyone two feet away.

That poor dude didn't look like no kid from El Chuco I'd ever known, but I gotta hand it to him, he'd do anything he could to get us to put three sentences together in some sorta order that made sense. He was supposed to teach us public speaking, man, even though half the class would never be let out in public again, much less be invited to the local

Kiwanis Club to give no talk. That Mr. Angel—and I would say it like all the Anglos did just to get his goat and to hear the prissy way he'd correct me and say it like in Spanish— he was real green and we ground him up, specially me.

We didn't have to pretend too hard that we didn't give a shit what he was saying cause we were all zonked out on something, mostly Thorazine, which is like this elephant tranquilizer that makes your skin turn green in the sun and all your teeth fall out before your thirty-fifth birthday. Mr. Johnson's skin was greenest of all and he was probably Mr. Drool cause he was losing teeth right and left. We were all on that junk at one time or another. The nurse's aides that took care of us didn't want no discipline problems. That control shit again, man, all the white-coats got it. It was a real bondage and discipline place, man.

Besides the Texas-size pacifiers they gave us to keep us all stupid and obedient, they also gave us cigarettes. If we wiped our asses, we got cigarettes. If we held a spoon right, we got cigarettes. If we jerked off by ourselves, we got cigarettes. If you ever wanna go to a cancer factory, just trot on down to your local V.A. Hospital. I never smoked so much in my life or hacked up so many noogies.

If you didn't smoke, then TV was the reward. I can still see the faces of them guys that got to watch the tube for being good little boys. Total blanks, man, no expression, like beyond Thorazine. Even la Mollie would agree they were complete passive passives, man, mindless zombies on parade. They couldn't sleep cause they'd miss some show, they couldn't eat, they'd walk around bumping into things and growling at anything real that got in their way.

And that was our recovery program, man. Thorazine, nicotine, TV and Mr. Angel's Educational Therapy classes every

123

morning between 9 and 11 A.M. to keep us defenders of the country going. It was Alice in Locoland, man, what can I say? And no one was telling Louie nothing.

I remember that time and them people like we was all part of a cartoon that's showing on some channel of my brain that I don't wanna turn to but keep finding again anyway every once in awhile. When I do find it again, it's like it's all happening right now. I never seen so many white rabbits in my life, man. A coupla kids, young, early Vietnam were in there already who'd gone off the deep end and kept to themselves and looked real hateful at the rest of us. But my favorites were the old guys, the World War I and II vets, cause they had some interesting stories to tell and made out like they knew how come they killed other guys.

One dude who I started thinking about while I was leaning on Tomás' car with my leg about as useful as one of them sticks you get to mix your drinks with had only half a face. The other half was burned away during an attack on one of them islands not too far from the Japanese mainland. This happened to him about the same time the first A-bomb was dropped and the guy woke up a coupla weeks later convinced he was the first atom that split in two. Well, man, what else can you tell yourself if you're looking into a mirror for the first time and seeing what happened to your face? And this ain't even no horror movie. This is real life.

When I first saw him, he walked over sideways—the good side—to where I was melting into the seat cause they just gave me a shot, and he said real secret, "There's two of us, you know."

"Pleased to meet you both," I said. I was ready to play along. After all, I was in there too and not real sure what I was seeing or not seeing. And that's when he told me that he was the first atom to split in two and stop the fighting. That was the end of our first talk cause the tranque kicked in and I fell asleep right after he said that and when I came to he was gone, like he'd dissolved into the mushroom cloud.

About three weeks later, he came up to me in the TV room and said, "You passed out before I could tell you my names. I'm Larry and Bryant. We're black, and shine shoes for a living at the Albuquerque airport. It's been restored to what it was in the old days."

"Hey, Larry! Hey, Bryant!" I say, shaking his hand twice, naturally. "I'm from that parta the country, too. El Paso, Texas." I'm really starting to get into it, man, but I see that Larry and Bryant wanna get on with the speech they memorized.

"Before I split in two, I was a blonde lesbian from Little Rock, Arkansas. All my friends called me Marilyn." He gave me a look straight outta *Gentlemen Prefer Blondes* when he said it.

Well, this was getting to be too much—even for me—and I interrupted him and said, "Hey, man, face it. You're not seeing it the way it is."

"Way it is? Way it is?" he says, almost normal. "How do you know the way it is? You're just an ugly little Spic with no manners from some hick Texas border town and you can't even speak English. Isn't that the way it is?"

Well, I don't wanna get started beating up on the guy, cause what's to beat up? So I try the rational approach and tell him that in this country being two black guys is not much better'n being a dyke. "How come you didn't split up into two rich Anglos?" I asked him in a serious way.

"Don't bother me," he says. "I got enough on my minds," and he turns that side of his face that got erased so's he can't even see me.

About a month later, like nothing happened and we were friends forever, he did his crab walk over to where I was pitching horseshoes by myself and started giving me his "I can't decide what kind of 'bi' I am, Louie, help me out" routine. He was still into twos, man. Was he bicultural—Mexican and Anglo? Bilingual? "Shouldn't you just speak English in this country?" he asked me over and over. Bisexual? "I can't decide who has more fun fucking, men or women, Louie, what do you think?" Even binomial, man, like he was some math problem. "Can zero be part of a binomial, Louie?"

The guy was a real mess—lotsa brains and lotsa education, good at words and paralyzed by language. Which one should he speak? he wanted to know. He had all them memories and he jumbled em all up in his brain trying to find patterns that made sense. Like he said something and then took it away at the same time. It was weird following him into his bi-world where most everything was either this or that, just cause he said it was. He was always hungry, too, and ate while he talked and talked outta one side of his mouth. The other side was too burned to move.

I finally got real tired of hearing him say the same shit over and over and one day I said, "You know what, dude? or dudes? I think you're just hungry for mammary. Why don't you go get laid by someone, man, and leave me alone?"

Stead of getting mad that time, he laughed and kept saying "hungry for mammary" again and again. The next day he told me that's what he was gonna call his collection of personal essays soon as he got around to writing em down. I said, "Great. Just remember you're gonna talk about you and not me." I wonder now if he ever got around to putting his bi-world down on paper.

But Two-Face wasn't no more loony than some of the others in there. There was this Mr. Emerson, for example, who was about ninety years old and thought the world was divided into "the proponents of sweat" and "the proponents of no-sweat" and gave you a lecture about that without noticing you turned your ears off after the first twenty seconds. He wasn't too interesting except that he reminded me a little of Leila P. cause he had hairs growing on the end of his knobby nose. And there was one real slick salt-and-pepper-hair professor who was supposed to've taught at Harvard or some other big deal Eastern college before he went off to the war. When he came back to his history courses, he freaked out one day when somebody asked him about the Jews in Europe cause he couldn't face the Holocaust so he denied it ever happened. And he don't deny it quietly, man, he yelled at anybody that brought up the subject, screaming at em that the Holocaust was a lie invented by Russia and the United States to drive all the Jews in the world crazy.

But Mr. Johnson'll always be my favorite. He musta belonged to that group of World War II guys but I don't know for sure cause he never said nothing to nobody. I ain't sure he even saw us with them milky-blue bloodshot eyes that only stared straight ahead. Naturally, I felt close to him right away cause he made me think about Evelina back home. The aide who took care of him let me sit next to him in E.T. He so broke my heart, man, that I knew I had it back. I'd put it in the freezer when Juan disappeared into the wild blue. And even though I never wanted to thaw it out again, I felt it start up every time I seen that aide's hand going towards that Big Swede's face. I lit cigarettes for him, which made all the other guys tease him and me and call us asshole buddies and lotsa junk like that, but I didn't care.

Mr. Johnson was bringing me back to life just by being there so's I could see how well off I was.

Maybe what I liked about him most, though, was how he could just be where he was drooling away in his chains like some spring and not make a move to answer to nobody but himself. That poor Angel kid would try everything to get us going in them classes of his and we'd try this or that or act sarcastic, but none of it'd touch Mr. Johnson. I gotta hand it to the Kid, though, he never gave up. Like once he got some of the guys interested in a parts of speech game, even me, though I didn't let on, of course. We were supposed to act out what part of speech we were. Or if we wanted, like him, we could dress up like a phrase or word that was connected to talking.

You know what he did? Outta one of them grocery bags, he pulled out a pink nylon slip and put it on over his shirt and pants. He was wearing a tie so he looked even funnier. Naturally, the minute I seen the slip, I got my usual reaction cause I ain't seen one for awhile and it took me a coupla minutes to get over it and remember this was a guy I was looking at and start figuring out a way to ruin his game.

"Guess what I am," Mr. Angel was saying with a smile cause he saw how shocked some of the guys were. "I'm a psychological phrase," he adds, giving us the big clue.

One of the aides raised her hand and said, "I know, I know," real excited, like we weren't supposed to think it was all planned. "You are a Freudian slip."

"Very good," he says. And then he wrote lotsa phrases and parts of speech on the board and told us to choose one and act it out like him. He said we could look through his bag for things to wear if we wanted.

Well, some of the guys got into it and started playing

adverbs and pronouns and conjunctions. But when Mr. Emerson kept putting on this silly hat in ways and places where no hat oughta be, I was getting sick of all the cutesy stuff. Kid Angel said he knew what Mr. Emerson was, but he kept everybody else guessing til he decided to tell us real dramatic, "A misplaced modifier!"

That made me really sick, but by then I'd figured out what I was gonna act out. I stood up, unzipped my pants and took it out. That shut everybody up. "Well, ain't no one gonna guess what part of speech this is?" I asked. And before anyone could answer, I said, "A dangling participle," put it back in, zipped up and sat down.

I gotta hand it to the Kid, though, cause he recovered pretty quick and right after I sat down he said, "That was very interesting, Mr. Mendoza. I wonder how you would have acted out a split infinitive?" And he gave me a pirate's smile that made me wanna smile back. But I didn't cause I didn't want none of the men to think I was a sissy like him.

One of them mornings about half-way through my time there, the Kid brought two grocery bags fulla spices, fruits and vegetables to E.T. He told us he wanted us to touch and smell what he was gonna pass around. He asked us not to taste—already, I took a big bite outta the apple and was chewing away—or to tell him what we heard, just in case any of us schizos heard anything. He said that after I announced out loud that the cantaloupe wanted me to do something nasty to it. The Kid was smiling so much, I figured he musta got laid the night before.

That day he was talking about poetry and telling us that our five senses were the beginning of poetry. I knew then and there for sure he was studying something totally useless and was gonna remain a poor Mexican from El

Chuco the rest of his life. But I gave him the benefit and just let him go on. He told us that if we really put our minds to it, we could come up with the essence of whatever it was we were smelling or touching. Man, I started getting the chills in my back cause it was like old Leila P. Harper was in the room grinning away and warning me to pay good attention to what was in front of my nose.

"Everyone can be a poet," the Kid was telling us suckers. "But most of us are too tired or too sick or too lazy to find the poet inside and so we spend our lives in a doormat stage waiting for something outside ourselves to give us life."

"I ain't no doormat," I said real loud.

"No, you're not, Mr. Mendoza," he said real bright. "You may be many things, but you are definitely not a doormat." I'm grinning and looking around to see if the guys are appreciating the fact. "But I didn't say 'doormat,'" the Kid goes on. "I said *dormant.*" He told us what that meant and I had to agree—in that room anyways, most everyone was pretty much asleep.

Somewheres in the farthest, smallest cell of my wacko brain, I heard Don Manuel's vibes, don't ask me how, and the shivers started coming in waves. Well, naturally I pretended nothing was going on and that what the Kid was saying was just a big load of caca. I made like I didn't wanna play along, but when the bottle of sage got around to me, the whole desert in bloom came outta nowhere—I could actually see it, man, no lie—and I was six years old again telling la Pixie I was gonna go out and play.

"Tell us what you're feeling, Mr. Mendoza," the Kid said in a real quiet voice, not wanting to interrupt what he musta seen was happening to my brain.

Me, I was Mr. Dumb, not able to say nothing and just

staring at the sage all purple against the wall separating the projects from the Border Highway. "That's all right, Mr. Mendoza. Just hold onto that feeling and when you can think of the words to describe it, tell us about it."

When I told la Mollie this story, she said I was lying cause Freud said that kinda thing was impossible and that no one could bring up an entire childhood outta just one smell. I told her I didn't care about what no weenie doctor said, cause the inside of his nose was all enamelled on coke anyways. I know what I was smelling and how I felt, and for the first time since I got to that forgetting place, the feeling was real.

But real ain't easy, man, ever, and I wasn't gonna let no Stanford fairy know he could get to me with some spice in a jar. "I know," I said, making myself come outta my desert dream. "It smells like Texas Ranger armpit juice." And everybody laughed that unreal laugh except the Kid, who didn't say nothing and just looked at me and went on passing around stuff from his bags.

Next to me, Mr. Johnson was holding on real tight to an avocado and not letting no one take it away from him. It's a good thing it weren't ripe or Mr. Johnson woulda had guacamole all over his hands. The guy on the other side of him kept elbowing him to pass it on. Nobody ever touched Mr. Johnson, man, he could kill.

"Leave him alone," the Kid said, real authoritative. "Keep passing around the other things and tell us what you feel." He started writing down what the guys said on the blackboard like they was lines of poetry.

There we were—a buncha grown crazy dudes—feeling fruits and vegetables, putting our noses into spice bottles like they was poppers, oohing and aahing away, and saying things like "This peach feels like April—April Dawn, the stripper at Prince Matchabelli's topless club," and "This carrot is my dick, hard and dirty," and like Mr. Emerson, who was holding onto a tomato and a zucchini, "I'm going to squash this tootsie tomato. Get it, boys?" We were coming up with all kindsa other lines that were getting funnier and funnier til we were all laughing—even the Kid—*real* laughter. Probably for the first time since they got back from wherever some of these guys done their killing or seen men they cared about get slaughtered. All of em laughing except, of course, Mr. Johnson. He sat there with great big Thorazine tears rolling down his pitted, greenish face and with the avocado in both his hands like he was holding an egg—real gentle, I could feel it. So could the aide, cause she stopped wiping his face.

Then, right in the middle of the hubbub, a silence—like the kinda silence you get when it snows in the desert and there ain't no wind—fell on one man after another when each of us seen that Mr. Johnson was trying to say something. He finally got it out in a real high-pitched voice like some phantom from an old, long, and tragic opera, spacing out each sound in the word like it was the last sound on earth.

"Ah. Voh. Cah. Doh. Ah-voh-cah-doh!" He made it seem like each syllable was a Mayan god. He did it once, real slow and quiet like he knew what he was holding in his hands, and the second time, real loud and quick in a shriek like he was finding gold.

For one long moment, all the guys woke up and nobody moved or talked—not even me—til some smart aleck started clapping in a real sarcastic way and the rest of us sheep joined in and the spell was broken for all eternity and a extra day. The Kid was trying not to cry outta frustration or happiness, I couldn't tell which. And Mr. Johnson went back into himself like a giant turtle that never stuck its head outta the shell cause someone was always there to whack it, hard. But it was a great moment, man, and I gotta admit that I choked up a lot and cried later for all the coo-coos in that place, specially Mr. Johnson.

And I was crying again, standing there in that cream-of-mushroom night waiting for my leg to get back on friendlier terms with my brain, and wishing that Big Swede was there so's he could carry me home to la Mollie, and wondering what he really saw through those bleached blue eyes of his.

Naturally, whenever I see an avocado now, I thinka Mr. Johnson. They finally locked him up for good cause the aide that took care of him quit during a wage dispute and nobody else wanted to risk being chained to him.

A coupla years later, the Angel Kid got asked to leave cause he spent one whole class playing Bob Dylan songs for the men and the Head Nurse decided he was a communist. If you ever wanna do some guys dirt, let it out that they're commies or queers—even if it ain't true—cause in this country, that's the worst thing anybody can be. So that was the end of him and the E.T. classes at the V.A. Hospital for the Hopeless.

I also found out the Kid had to have a operation that saved his life but left him with a bag of shit at his side for the rest of his stay in this world. Man, I'm telling you, them poetry teachers sure get the fuzzy end of the lollipop. I love it when Marilyn says that line in *Some Like It Hot*. It makes me wanna protect her forever.

CHAPTER V

Just Like Romeo and Juliet

I ain't one to give up on things too easy, but leaning there against my brother's car with the pain shooting through my leg like one of them tracer bullets, I woulda given a lot for someone to tuck me in. It was the first time since they let me outta that V.A. loony bin that I missed it and wished I was back there chewing up pills like they was steak and sleeping my days away. I was gonna need more than Mr. Johnson's avocado to get me home to la Mollie's arms. I figured Tomás'd be my ticket if I could just find him in that after-hours joint up the alley. With about ten more motorcycles parked in the alley and what seemed like all the leather queers this side of New York buzzing around the door of the place, I shoulda had some clue what was going on in there, but I wasn't thinking so clear. I headed down the alley, keeping myself together by saying the names of some of them sweet breads la Pixie used to buy at the Aracataca Bakery on the corner of Florence and Paisano Drive.

There are two important buildings in every barrio, man—the church and the bakery. Whenever I felt a lotta pain, I used to say bread names like a rosary. I been doing it for what seems like forever. It always used to make the guys in the gang laugh, though some of em coulda used their own homemade mantra, all cut up after a skirmish against the Fatherless Gang. The draft took care of mosta that, though there are still forty- and fifty-year-old gang members hanging around El Chuco. Them old Ace of Spades brothers still got their heads in the same place, man. And the younger guys' heads are all messed up with drugs. It's just ugly. Nothing stays the same, except them Mexican sweet breads.

That Aracataca baked magic. Mr. and Mrs. García got the bakery after her parents died and kept all the old recipes. They were good people. La Pixie knew the family real well so we got special treatment and free extras whenever we went there.

We never could figure out which one did the baking. One day she was out helping the customers and the next we saw him. Mrs. García looked like a pharmacist in a starched white apron and her hair pulled back in a bun. He looked like a *chamuco*—that's my favorite Mexican sweet bread, man, and there ain't no English word for it. He had a thick moustache and these big dark eyes that were always gleaming like he knew some secret we all needed to get into heaven, and it was gonna come to us in the very next bite. Maybe that's why at Christmas time he always played one of them Magi.

I wish I could tell you the names of them sweet breads in Spanish, man, cause changing em to English makes em lose their flavor. Don't get me wrong, neither. I think everybody needs to know English to get by in this country—the real English, not that liar's language the businessmen, lawyers, and politicians use. Don't even get me started on those dollar-bill words and sentences we're supposed to learn cause it ain't English. I'm glad Miss Harper ain't around no more to hear it. I know she'd say it was deader than Latin and nowheres near as beautiful. I even like Shakespeare's language better than that gobbledygook. Now that's a word, man. La Mollie taught it to me. Sounds like a description of turkey shit.

I don't want everybody to speak like me—that would be boring—but I don't want no one telling me I can't talk this way neither. And all this caca about which is the real mother tongue—our language is accents, man, like Virgil's and yours and mine. There's only one language that counts anyway. Ain't you gonna ask me what that is? The language of the heart, man, and most times you don't even need words to speak it.

That was the way them Garcías talked, man, with their hearts. Their bakery smelled like music. Right away you opened the door and took a whiff you left reality. Them smells was a jungle of delight—gingerbread pigs came out steaming on a tray, the egg bread knew exactly how far to rise, the Mexican rolls tasted better than any sourdough I ever ate.

The Garcías was wizards, man, and they could turn plain old flour, milk, and sugar into sweet breads called *novias, libros,* and *campechanas.* Get this. Them names mean "brides," "books," and "little old ladies you can talk to about your problems." Ain't that a kick? I love them names as much as the tastes of the bread.

So while I'm gimping over to the entrance of this Harley joint looking for Marlon Brando and his gang from *The Wild One,* I'm saying my Mexican sweet bread prayer to get me there. "*Chamuco . . . Laberinto . . . Pedo de monja . . .*" And so on. I already told you about the first name. The second you can figure out. That third one means "nun's fart," man, ain't that something? And it's called that cause it's a real delicate, paper-thin tube that's filled with lotsa white goo. I never liked to eat em too much, but I sure got a lotta mileage outta the name. La Mollie, of course, don't believe that any bread would be called that. I wish I could tell you all the names, man. Too bad you only know English.

So taste by taste I'm getting to the front door of that place, which as I get closer I can see is called The Mind Shaft and where I'm deciding all the motorcycle fairies in San Francisco must be having their after-hours coffee and seeing who they're gonna hit on to help em make it through the night. I'm praying that Tomás is gonna be sitting at a table right near the front door so's I don't have to walk around giving everyone the wrong idea. Like I told you, man, I can't even think about sex without tits around. Real soft ones.

I got a friend named Lou and she knows what I mean. She's always teasing me and telling me I'm nothing but a lesbian trapped in the body of a macho man. Hell, man, I admit it. I love the taste of women. Lou was married and had three kids before she looked real close at herself and saw that where she wanted to be was with another woman. Her husband wasn't around too much anyways, so she took the kids and found this lady Sarah within two years. They're out in the Sunset district cause Lou wanted her kids to go to old-fashioned neighborhood schools and get that basic readin', writin', and 'rithmetic stuff. And she's had a good life with Sarah for almost twenty years now. Sarah is one of them gourmet cooks and even though la Mollie naturally don't understand two women making it with each other, whatever she pretends about it, she loves the way Sarah makes us this stuff you never even seen in restaurants and serves it to us on a plate that looks like a painting. To me, all that stuff tastes just like it looks, but I love them women cause they take care of each other.

I'm limping like a dog that just got it from some car by the time I get to the door of The Mind Shaft. There's this short, fat guy with a scruffy beard taking money and pushing back the crowd waiting to get in. I ain't got but a few coins in my pocket and I'm not about to give them away.

"One dollar," the fat guy says, pretending not to notice the way I'm dragging my leg.

"Hey, man, I just wanna see if my little brother's in there. I need a ride home."

This guy is even more round up close and looks like a ball in drag with handcuffs on the side. He looks down at my leg, then right into my face. I don't want him to think I'm interested in bouncing him up and down, but I know enough to look back real vulnerable.

"Sweetheart," he says in a Bogie voice, "we're all looking for our little brothers when we're not looking for Daddy. Go on in but I'm only giving you twenty minutes to find him and then I'm coming after you myself." He says something to somebody behind this big black vinyl curtain and then looks at me real hard one more time.

"Are you a cop?" he asks me.

"Me? Hell no, man. I hate the fuzz." I act real injured that he would even ask me that question.

"Too bad," he says all serious. "Cop types are my biggest turn-on. Leave your driver's license or drop your pants and show me your collateral," he says, like they're the same thing. "Your choice."

I dig out my license and leave it with him. "Cute picture," he says, and pulls the vinyl curtain aside so's I can go in.

I can tell pretty quick this ain't no pajama party at Hernando's Hideaway. There's a bar with a coupla guys drinking stuff outta styrofoam cups that glow in the blacklight. I don't see no tables or chairs, just benches along the sides where a buncha dudes are sitting or standing. Mosta the guys don't have hardly no clothes on, except for a couple in the corner dressed like Marines and one cowboy standing at the bar with his ten-gallon hat down low over his face. The only thing I can tell for sure is who's wearing contact lenses cause the light makes em glow green in the dark. I hate blacklight, man—it's even creepier than the lights in here. The whole place smells like leather and Clorox and guys working out in a gym. Sorta like the men's room in the Cathedral High swimming pool in El Chuco, man, where me and my buddies used to terrorize them middle-class Chicanas from Sister Abigail's catechism class.

Not even *cucuys* would walk into this place, man, and there I am clunking my cast across the room and trying not to have no one notice. I don't see Tomás nowheres and I probably wouldn't reconnize him if I did unless he talked to me. I do one of them Wild Bill Hickoks and go for a corner where my back's covered. I figure I'm pretty safe where the bar meets one wall and nobody can get behind me unless they force it.

There's some real loud disco music coming from the next room with a coupla minutes of opera shit thrown in. Disco ain't music to me, man. It's nothing but electronic noise with a lotta screaming, and I hate it even more than opera. But after about a minute I figure out that what I'm hearing ain't coming outta no speakers. What I thought was a disco beat now's sounding more like somebody getting whipped, and that opera screeching is making me think of people dying. And not soon enough to suit me, man.

The guys reeling in from the other room are real sweaty and panting just a little. Most of em don't even bother to put no clothes back on. I'm starting to catch on that they ain't just dancing in there and I just hope Tomás don't got no part in it, cause no way am I gonna leave my spot against the wall to go next door and look for him. I'm beginning to be glad that la Pixie ain't alive to see that her boys spend their nights lost in some south-of-Market Babylon for fairies.

Somebody has sent me this icy mug of beer and even though I could use one right now more than a foot rest, I don't even leave a fingerprint in the frost. I don't look up to see who the bartender points to as my benefactor, and I just barely have the nerve to take a peek at the guy that's standing next to me. I don't remember that he was there before. I'm sure I woulda noticed, cause what I see just about does me in, man. He's all naked except for a pair of boots, a cowboy hat, and about a dozen clothespins clamped onto diffrent parts of his body, even down there, where I never dreamed I would see one.

We used to have some pretty crude initiation ceremonies in our gang, man, but nothing like this. We only pretended we were gonna hurt guys where it hurts the most— we never actually did it. This dude made me thinka them stories about Indian tribes and the kindsa rituals they put young bucks through before they'd make it to manhood. He made me forget all about my own pain just thinking about what it must feel like to be pinched like that in the you-know-what. He noticed the look on my face and asked real matter-of-fact, "Are you into pain?"

"Actually," I tell him, trying to sound just as casual and like I don't really care what's going on or what he's got on, "my leg hurts like hell. I just broke it."

"Oh, too bad. You're serious. I thought that was your costume for the night and that you were just looking for some-

141

one to play doctor. I thought it was pretty clever and told myself I might try that next time so I could get somebody in this hole to notice me." He's telling me all this as calm as calm can be, sipping from a beer bottle and looking towards the vinyl curtain and not missing nobody that walks in. "I like doctor scenes, especially when they include water sports."

"What're water sports?" I ask him. I need to hang onto words cause I'm starting to really see and hear and smell what's going on around me. I feel about as ignorant as Sonia's mom in that confessional, man. Oh, Virgil, where are you now?

I like to think there ain't nothing I can't say, but I ain't gonna talk about that Mind Shaft. I'm only gonna tell you that them dudes weren't just standing and sitting around chit-chatting. They were getting right down to business there in front of everybody like it was the most natural thing in the world, and I'm thinking I better get outta there before I do run into Tomás and embarrass him and me. But I'm telling you, man, what them sissies can take is more than any straight guy I ever known could take or would want to. I gotta hand it to them fruits—they can handle pain better than me.

"You don't know about water sports?" Mr. Clothes-pins asks me with a real amused look on his face, the first expression I seen on it since we started talking. "Come on in the back. They have a water sports room here. I'll show you what they are."

Well, I figure he ain't talking about no tubs and rubber duckies and so I stay as cool as I can. "No thanks," I say. "Maybe next time." And I start thumping my way back to the door cause I'm hearing the twenty-minute clock ticking away and I can see Mr. Ball's head peering around the vinyl curtain looking for me.

I wanted to make a quick exit, or as quick as I could manage in my condition, so naturally I tripped and bumped into guys all the way out. I started sweating real heavy like everybody else there and then, at the door, I ran right into Mr. Ball's round, round belly.

"It's real hot in here," I tell him, not knowing what else to say except what's under my nose. And outta nowhere he's blowing three breaths, real quick and real cool and not bad smelling neither, right into my sweaty face. They kept me from passing out, man, I really believe it, cause I was on the edge. I shoulda thanked him probably but all I wanted to do was get my license and fade away.

"Did you find your little brother?" he asks, like he really cares.

"No, but that's okay. I'll find a way to get back home. Don't worry about it." I'm feeling real uncomfortable about everything, man.

"Well, honey," Mr. Ball says, giving me the once over and squeezing my biceps. "If I wasn't on duty, I'd take you home. I can play little brother real good and wouldn't mind showing you how good it can be. Or how bad, if that's what you're into."

"Thanks," I tell him. "But I got a woman waiting for me."

He lets out a big whoop, louder than the opera singer, who's still screeching away, and helps me hang on to the slippery curtain—there was grease all over it, man—to keep from tripping. At the door he tells me real confidential, "That's what they all say when they look in the mirror, baby. You come back soon."

Maybe I didn't hear him right cause I was fighting with that stupid curtain, but I been thinking about what he said about looking in the mirror and I can't come up with what he meant.

"Yeah, sure," I tell him, not knowing what to say. "Thanks, man." The fresh air hits my lungs like a baseball bat.

Fast as my leg lets me, I move on down to the end of the block. All outta breath and trying real hard not to pass out, I sit on the curb, put my head on my knees, and wait for my soul to drive by and pick me up, cause I was more tired than I ever been in my life. That dumb comet was making me look at things I ain't never seen or ever wanna see again.

When I was making all them phone calls this morning trying to keep the *cucuys* away before you and your listening machine showed, I called Tomás to tell him where I was and I asked him about them sports. He laughed real loud and told me I didn't wanna know.

"I seen your car near that place, Tomás. Were you there?" The big brother in me couldn't keep from asking.

"It's none of your business, Louie," he says real tough. "But if you want to know, no, I wasn't. I loaned my car to a friend and as a matter of fact, he hasn't brought it back. Maybe he's still there."

I was relieved. I wanted to tell him how it really was with la Mollie but I knew I'd start crying and then he'd start worrying about me and I didn't wanna upset him. So I told him she was doing okay and that we was just waiting to get the release papers and some pills for her pain.

"I can go get groceries for you and Mollie," he said. "Just tell me what you need."

"No, it's okay. We'll stop at the Safeway on the way home." I was trying to be real light but I could tell he knew something was going on.

"Well, let me know," he said. "And Louie, forget about the water sports, okay? Cause if you ask me about them again, I'm going to tell you what they are. You won't like it.

Call me if you need anything."

"I will," I told him, but I didn't wanna be asking him for help right then cause I was still so sad about what I'd seen in that bar. I needed Virgil Spears to talk to me about this, man. I know he coulda told me how come them guys needed to get into each other's guts like that. And I was thinking about Tomás, too, and having a real hard time figuring out how he lived his life. I didn't hate him or feel disgusted, just real sorry, man, sorta like my heart'd been busted by that drum stead of my shin.

I kept seeing pictures of all them dudes connected to each other in these weird ways, like their bodies were machines and could be bent and stretched in all directions. Nobody was laughing, neither—just making noises like the kind people make when they ache or want something. Kinda like being hungry, only the kinda hunger you feel when you ate plenty but you're still starving. Like there's lotsa food in front of you on the table and you don't really wanna eat no more, but you just put the nearest goodie in your mouth and chew away til it's gone anyways. And then you find the goodies are still there even after you eat em, so you start again.

It was eerie, man—not *cucuy* eerie but human eerie— and I reconnized the old demon lust winking in the back-ground of all them pictures I couldn't erase from my head. That monster was the one putting oil all over that vinyl curtain, I'm sure of it. I had to keep telling myself that it was only a buncha guys doing all that stuff and not no ex-traterrestrials. Maybe the whole thing felt strange to me cause there weren't no women around and women always bring something mysterious into any room. They don't even have to say nothing. Just one woman in a room fulla guys will change everything. Ever notice that?

145

I still don't know what it was that got in my skin about that place, but it had me stuck there in the alley so's I couldn't of moved if Sherman's army'd showed up. I sat on the curb breathing deep til the world began to turn to the sun again and that white soft light before dawn chased any ghosts or *cucuys* around the block and back to where they came from. There wasn't even any fairies on the street by that time. I was alone, just sitting and breathing. I knew then that my soul weren't coming for me in no stretch limo, man. I had to go and claim it. So after awhile I got up and tried putting some weight on the broken leg. It hurt but I knew I could make it as far as Market Street and catch the trolley that would take me outta this end-of-the-world night.

You can count on Market Street to be there, man, cutting across San Pancho from the Ferry Building to Twin Peaks. We call them peaks *las chi-chis,* so you can figure out what that makes Market Street. Market don't care that the streets that run into it are forced to make ninety-degree turns and still keep the same name. If that confuses everybody, that ain't its fault. It just goes its own way, man, and lets the rest of the town readjust.

You know what? I think the earth gods put San Francisco on a fault line to keep it from ever getting too stuck on itself. Anything that beautiful would get spoiled real fast without nothing to threaten it. To lotsa people, San Francisco is a beautiful woman floating face-up on the Pacific. When she ain't floating, man, she walks on water and turns into clouds carrying you along. She's better than a fairy-tale city, specially in the morning when the earth and the light are meeting again after being separated so long by the night. Then she shines in the sun with a tender glow.

Down on the flat part of Market Street near the Tenderloin, where I dragged myself onto it like a injured wet rat on a dry drunk, I could start making out the winos. They were stretched out against doorways where the warm air coming through the cracks from inside them big buildings kept em from catching pneumonia. Some of the real old people that live in them run-down hotels between Mission and Market were out for their stroll of the day cause dawn's the safest time for em to take it. A couple of em across the street looked like fat birds all wrapped up in Salvation Army coats. Others just looked like slow-moving bundles of blankets. One of them little old ladies took one look at me clunking towards her and said, real cheery like she knew me, "Good morning. You look like you had a real good time, you handsome devil," and she passed on by, like an owl on its way to some church in the branches. Them old people are the real extraterrestrials, man. Most of em are ready for outer space. Anything's better than living on Social Security in one of them rooms in the Anglo Hotel.

The Muni stop is your world's headquarters for trashy newspapers, man, with one vending machine after another lined up all along the street. And that morning la Mollie coulda written the headlines for em all: WORLD ENDS TODAY, and COMET TO COLLIDE WITH EARTH, and THE END IS HERE, KAHOUTEK KONQUERS; with a "k"—not too bad, you know. I like "k's." I didn't have no extra change to buy one for la Mollie and still pay for the ride back to her, even though I wanted to let her read about it before it happened. The first coupla paragraphs I could see through them little vending windows don't tell me more than what I know already from la Mollie, but it was like them newspapers were glad the world was gonna end.

I don't get it. It's scary, man, the way a lotta people

really believe we're all gonna get blown up so why bother. Since it says right there in the Bible that it's gonna happen, they spend all their time getting prepared stead of thinking about if they might be able to change things. I think they're making it happen, man, living their lives waiting for the end like that. I wonder if they're gonna have time to say "I told you so" when the first missile or comet or whatever hits em.

I didn't even look to see what the headline on the *Chronicle* was. That paper's just one giant cartoon. The ones in El Paso ain't no better, but at least they don't pretend to care about what's going on in the rest of the world, and their letters to the editor are a lot more fun cause every one they print is written by some wacko survivalist high on patriotism or on some candy cane picture of Jesus.

But a coupla minutes before the Judah Street trolley opens its doors to let me in, I'm standing behind some guy who's holding up the *Chron* in front of his face. And he's reading something about a high school girl in the East Bay who was saved by the heart of the boyfriend she turned down. He managed to off himself just to will her his heart so she'd never reject him again and they'd go on ticking away their days together forever. I tell you, life and the *Chronicle* come up with some doozies. I started wondering how the old boyfriend managed to kick the bucket just to convenience her.

"Musta been a Mexican," I said to the driver, who just ignored me and was only interested in seeing I put exactly the right amount of change into the collecting machine. Only a Mexican can love like that. Even if you reject me, I'll still die for you and see that you get my fresh and pounding heart so's you can go on to other lovers. It comes from our Aztec background, man, and all them sacrifices we made to get the sun to come up every day. We knew it wouldn't do it without us.

There was only two old guys in long black coats on the bus and they're sitting near the rear exit and looking like they just came from a flashers' convention. I gotta confess that I mighta seen anything then I was so delirious from being so tired and the feeling that I was finally on my way back home. Unless Kahoutek hit us before we got through the tunnel, I was gonna hold my sweet sweet honey close to me again.

The trolley moved like one of them slow-motion shots of a marshmallow melting above a low flame. It stopped at every single corner like it was waiting for permission to cross the street. Once, it got unhooked from its connection and the driver got out to fix it and everything else that was wrong on the planet Earth. It took him ten hours to get back in. And when I finally got off and hit the sidewalk just two blocks from la Mollie's bed, I heard something snap near my left hip.

But I was too close to worry about that none. Them blocks was definitely life in dream-time, man. Every love scene in every movie I ever saw went running through my head in wavy ripples that made me feel like I been drinking again and didn't know where or how or what. The scenes and the characters and the movie stars got all mixed up, and I was playing in em all. It was a giant Mexican mural of Hollywood starring me, Louie Mendoza, of course!

I was Rhett Butler saying goodbye to Scarlett and asking her to kiss me like she was sending me off to war. I could feel the sting of her slap across my face. I was even that flake Ashley Wilkes coming back to Tara with Melanie running towards him down the road. I got the goose-bumps,

man. Then I was Rick in Paris with the Kid, and then looking at her at the Casablanca airport, their two big hats kissing each other above their eyes cause they couldn't never
kiss each other's lips again. That movie is the love story of
them two hats, man.

I was Paul Henried handing Charlotte Vale a whole
branch of camellias, then lighting both their cigarettes, handing her one over and over til they both took a puff and the
smoke came between them like sex. Nicotine addicts in love.
I turned into Gregory Peck and Jennifer Jones hunting each
other down in the desert and killing their passion cause it
was too hot for them to handle. The desert faded into a
jungle and I was Tarzan swimming towards Jane with Cheeta
on the shore doing back-flips and going into a chimpanzee
ecstasy.

Right as I reached the bottom of the front steps— miracle
of movie miracles—everything and everybody dissolved into
Elizabeth Taylor's eyes. Them eyes are the reason the movies were invented, man. There I was, Monty Clift before his
accident, looking into them and hearing Angela Vickers say
in the biggest and greatest all-time close-up ever, "Come to
Momma. Come to Momma." I thought my heart was gonna
jump outta my chest and rush up them stairs ahead of me.

I put the key in the door real quiet and got my leg in
without banging it on nothing. It musta been about 7 or 8
a.m. so I thought la Mollie was still asleep upstairs. I didn't
know nothing about her night and what she found out, or
thought she did, about what happened at Big Eddie's.

After all I'd been through, I didn't wanna try and call
out cause I wanted her to see me first in all my glory. But I
needed a drink of water real bad before I tried climbing the
stairway to heaven and her, so I made my way slow and

quiet to the kitchen at the end of the hall, dragging that cast along the floor so's it seemed to whisper.

When I got there, man, I saw la Mollie standing at the sink. She had her back to me and was in that see-through robe she had on a million hours ago back yesterday morning, with that pink skin of hers showing all hazy through the gauzy stuff. She was looking into them dishes piled up in the sink like she'd lost something. I could tell she was hanging on to the front of the porcelain real tight, like for dear sweet life, but still I didn't know why. All I could see was that I'd made it back to my woman, where I never wanted to leave again. Even Elizabeth Taylor's eyes weren't nothing to la Mollie's back shining at me through that shady wrapper of hers.

"Honey," I said, real soft and then, when she didn't turn around right away, a little louder, thankful sorta, almost like a prayer, "Honey." It seemed like the word had to vault this huge wall of glue that was between me and her. It seemed like she kept getting farther and farther away off into the horizon every step I took getting closer to her. It seemed like I was walking so slowly toward the sink a turtle coulda hit the water first.

But she started to shake when she heard me, and when she turned, her face went from creamy to ghost white. Her beautiful hands flew up to her heart and she fell backwards. She dropped like a shot—just crumpled, fell into herself like some brick building meeting the wrecking ball. I was back in slow-motion land again, reaching out to her inch by inch like Cary Grant trying to touch Eva Marie Saint before she slides down Mt. Rushmore, when I see la Mollie go down and hit the back of her head against the edge of the sink. The blood started pouring out like a fountain gone bonkers, but the whole thing don't register til I hear the chunk of her skull. It was another one of them awful moments in life.

I don't know how I got her and me into that stupid car of hers that her daddy picked off the biggest lemon tree in the western hemisphere. And I don't know how I got the thing to start first time. But even that car musta known I'd had enough trouble for one night. I wrapped a roll of paper towels around la Mollie's neck and put another roll behind her head like a pillow. She was out cold but breathing regular, and I just wanted her to stop bleeding cause that much blood gave me the creeps, man. I didn't wanna think of no one dead or dying. Everything I did was in that kinda calm people get into, who knows how, when they know Death is knocking at the door and maybe even got a skeleton key and they gotta pretend with all their might that they ain't hearing nothing. But God, I was so scared. Every time I looked over at la Mollie, she was turning another shade of pale. That fucker Death, king of the *cucuys,* was breathing down my baby's neck.

I didn't call out her name or nothing cause I didn't want Death to even think I was fighting for her. That's an argument nobody on this side of the grave ever wins. I'm Mexican, man, and Death ain't no beautiful woman to me. He's a skeleton with a great big grin. I wanted *Señor Calavera* to believe that whatever he was doing was okay by me so's he would think la Mollie was nothing special and leave her alone this time around. The Big Creep has taken more than his share of the people I love.

This one line of poetry jumped into my head, and I kept saying it again and again, not even remembering where it was from or where I had run across it. "And yet I wish but for the thing I have . . . And yet I wish but for the thing I have." Over and over, faster even then I do them sweet bread names from the Aracataca, til the words lost any meaning and it seemed I was turning into some kinda Holy Roller speaking in tongues dropped on him by the Holy Ghost. It was a new rosary for me, man, and I got lost in it. Anyone seeing or hearing me woulda called the men in little white coats right then and there. But this was San Francisco.

About halfway to hell with me driving like I'm in some kind of Keystone Cops caper, la Mollie's eyes snapped open. It was like whatever had left her rushed back in and took over again and she let herself look across the seat at me. She was back from the land of the Dead, man, but only part-way. And I wanted to let her know she had to keep coming without tipping off the Bone Man that I cared. "Don't move your head," I told her. "I'll faint." I meant she would, of course, but I didn't know what I was saying I was so glad to see the color of her eyes one more time. Even her hair started coming back to normal. We were sitting at a stop light on Dolores and Sixteenth. I wanted to run it but couldn't cause the two cars in fronta me weren't budging, even though I was honking and hollering and acting like King Kong trying to break outta his chains.

"You're alive," la Mollie said real crystal clear. She looked at me like for the first time she knew it was really me and no ghost come back to haunt her forever.

"Of course I'm alive. What are you saying? Please stay still and don't talk."

Telling la Mollie not to talk is like telling me to wrap this up and let you get on to your other work. I promise you're only gonna need one more tape, man. In a coupla minutes more, if they don't bring her out here dancing I'm

153

gonna jump outta this seat and go find out what they're
doing with la Mollie cause I can't wait, whatever the matter
is. Anyways, I'm almost through. I fell for that lady cause
she's a talker like me and cause we're both scared shitless of
that creepy silent world most everybody walks around in.
The electricity ain't just in our bodies but in our mouths
mostly, hope you understand that. La Mollie and me are
word people and we keep our demons away by talking or
making music or making love. It's a good arrangement mosta
the time.

"They told me you were dead," she said, clear as a bell
with no crack in it. Then she passed out for about ten long,
long seconds. It was in that awful quiet that I asked God
not to let her die—I figured this was one of them last resort
moments. Then there was Evelina again.

She's standing on the street corner waiting for the light
to change. This time she don't look at me but just keeps
licking on a snow cone. She's wearing a summery dress with
lotsa bright flowers all over it and she looks all shiny and
healthy like she never lived or died. She seems about as far
away from pain as Oz is from Kansas.

I figured it was time for Errol Flynn, so I peeled around
them two cars in my way, flipped em off, and started speed-
ing towards Potrero. When la Mollie came to again, she
didn't stop talking til we got here, like she knew that long
as her mouth kept moving her ticker weren't gonna give up
neither. That's how come I know she thought I was in
nadaland flying around on rental wings, but now it was my
turn to worry about her ending up there all alone. I told her
we was all a-okay—even Emma—and la Mollie gave me
one of her million-dollar smiles and said she was real glad.

I brought her to this toilet cause I didn't know where

154

else to go. But the whole time I felt like I was walking towards that L.A. County emergency room again, looking for Evelina and hoping with every ounce of blood in my body that she was still alive. I was like some madman who don't know what to do or where to turn and ends up running right into Death. There ain't nothing left then, man, except cop to the fact that you're in for it, whatever way you been trying to fool the Big Spook and pretending to look back at them hollow eyeholes of his and not get sucked in.

Old Leila P. used to tell us that King Lear dies thinking that his good daughter is still alive and so he dies happy. But I knew better, man. Cordelia's too good to live on in any play Shakespeare'd write. I liked her cause she don't say too much and just goes around doing for others. I kinda liked the Fool, too, cause he don't pretend to make sense when he talks and of course makes the most sense of all. That dumb old man Lear? He was the King of Tears, man. Me, Chakespeare Louie from the projects, I know almost from the beginning of the story, even if him and Miss Harper don't, that the old king's daughter is as dead as a doornail at the end.

I don't want la Mollie to die on me but if she does, I sure hope I ain't gonna go around acting like that old man and pretending it never happened. Unless I'm really crazy and seeing la Mollie's breath mist over every mirror I look into. Then that old man Lear's gonna have to defend his throne cause I'm gonna cry so much that all the people'll be wanting to anoint *me,* whatever Miss Harper'd say to dissuade em. But you don't wanna hear about how much I can cry, do you? You want us Chicanos to be tough little Mexicans that got calluses on our scars and come outta the barrio with steel knuckles thinking the world's a prize fight,

155

right? That ain't how it is, man. Hurt's hurt, I don't care what you call it or how you say it. And if you been through enough of it, the only way to talk it out is all wet in tears.

All that's happened's made me punchy. I can't take no more of this waiting and waiting to hear about la Mollie and know if she's gonna live or if she's gonna be off in some coma meeting comets of her own or if she'll have to be a vegetable the rest of her life. Even the talking ain't holding back time no more, man. I ain't never been much of a waiter, and it's getting to me, let me tell you. I don't want her to die. That matters more than any of the caca I've been saying so far. I watched too many endings in my life and this ain't a story where I wanna see no last act.

You know, right before they wheeled her away on one of them ugly gurneys down that long dark hall, la Mollie came around one more time. She looked at me real hard and said, plain as can be, "I love you, Clark. I always have."

In a flash, when she said them words, I remembered where that rosary line in the car come from. It was Leila P. of course. Not her, I mean, but her main man Will. That woman. She coulda played the Wicked Witch or them harridans in *Macbeth* by the time she taught me. Old Fuzz-Face is what we used to call her, cause seemed like she had more hair all over her face than on her head. She was pretty wrinkled up and her hair was snow white. La Mollie has eyes like her, man, so blue they poke holes right through you.

But I learned a lot from that old lady. She used to bring diffrent sizes of them old wooden yarn spools painted all kindsa colors to class to stand for all them kings and queens and their buddies in Shakespeare. She'd set up a little stage on her desk by putting a piece of cardboard on top of two stacks of books with a space between the stacks to let some of the action go on under the cardboard, usually wars and stuff like that. Then she'd get all quiet. She wouldn't start til she could see everybody's face, and she'd glare at you til you realized you were the hidden one and moved your seat so's she could see that you had a good view of her stage.

If you dared to yawn in Leila P.'s class, she threw something at you—anything that she picked up first. One time I got a glass paperweight right in my lap and before I could complain that she almost robbed me of my manhood, she said, "If you chipped that, I'll keep you after school for a week, Louie." Leila P. was a toughie, let me tell you.

There was a story about her and that wooden leg of hers. We never knew if it was true but all of us wanted to believe it, so we just kept saying it long enough til it didn't matter if it'd really happened or not. When she was young, according to the legend, Leila P. Harper was a beautiful woman with red, red hair. She lost her leg when she was ice skating on a pond somewheres in Connecticut—which to me sounded like Siberia, U.S.A.—with the guy she was supposed to marry. They skated out too far and the ice cracked and both of em fell through. He drowned and she ended up an old maid with a wooden leg. She left her home and went to the desert to start a new life where nothing would remind her of that lost happiness. Least that's what we liked to think, even the guys—that Leila P. loved that guy too much to marry anyone else, so she just stayed on alone and became a high school English teacher. Naturally.

Sometimes, when I'd get real annoyed with her about something—it didn't take much—I liked to picture Leila P. sliding around on her back out there in the cold, her lover just an underwater memory, and only the wind making any sound, waving her arms and legs like a chicken on ice, not able to turn herself over. When it got really bad, I pushed both her and her skinny fiancé into the water myself and held em under til no more bubbles came up. I could thinka some terrible things to do to Miss Harper, worse than what life already done or would do to her.

Long time after I left El Chuco, I found out that Leila P. had slit her throat in some old peoples' home in Jal, New Mexico, then woke up in the County Hospital to find she had botched the job. She asked an attendant to give her some sleeping pills, took em all, and died of seizures cause she was allergic to whatever was in em. Someone shoulda gave her a trophy at the high school reunion, man. She went the Shakespeare way.

But I gotta admit I sorta miss that old lady, almost as much as la Pixie and my old man and Evelina. I don't know how come she put up with me. I fought her every step of the way cause I figured my mind was *my* turf. If there is any afterlife and I get to see her again, I know I'm gonna have to eat a lotta caca pie and make myself go and apologize to her the way I done to that tree. I'll probably cry in fronta her, too, but that's okay cause my heart hurts now when I thinka all them horrors I put her through in my head.

When she taught us the balcony scene from *Romeo and Juliet,* Leila P. herself chose the spools for the main characters. Mosta the time she let us do it, but when she had her favorites she told you what was what and you didn't talk back. Juliet was a small light-blue one and Romeo was a skinny tall wood-color one that nobody liked except Miss Harper. "Must remind her of the guy who got away, the lucky stiff," I said so's the guys and some of the girls could hear me. I wanted Romeo to be played by a red-colored spool cause to me, man, he's just another horny teenage guy. Is there any other kind? The play belongs to Juliet, anyways, not to him. She's the one that loses everything at the end you know. And for what? If Romeo had just waited a coupla more minutes, he woulda seen her come outta that death the monk made—there's that church again, man, they never leave you alone this side of the grave. Then the two of em coulda lived happily ever after next door to Will and his old lady in one of them weird cottages at Stratford-on-Avon that Miss Harper showed us pictures of. She even showed us that Chandos portrait of Shakespeare, which she said probably wasn't what the guy really looked like. Too bad, cause he looks kinda like a Chicano in that painting, man.

Anyways, Romeo and Juliet coulda had a buncha kids that threw spitwads at Mr. Kill-Everybody-Off every time he sat down to write another play about how to get along with the help of monks and nurses. Or about expecting some horny teenage guy to wait five minutes before making a life-and-death decision. But no. In less than two minutes, Romeo decides Juliet's dead, knows for sure that he ain't getting any from her again, ever, and lets himself have it. Not a dude to respect, man.

Leila P., dictator, made us write out in our own words what we thought the characters were saying. Mosta the time in Shakespeare, I didn't have no clue, man. No human being I never heard talked like them.

Anyways, I was always on the side of the gruntlings Miss Harper told us couldn't afford no tickets and just milled around on the ground in fronta the stage. I liked to think of em making farting noises, eating onion sandwiches, yelling and throwing things at the actors when they got bored with all them long speeches. I know I woulda been throwing tomatoes like mad. I think they had tomatoes in them olden days, man, but I don't know for sure, cause England ain't California and the sun don't shine too much there from what I hear. It's how come English people are all white, right? Except the ones they let in to do the dirty work from where they conquered and slaughtered everyone to make sure the sun never set on their little island.

But in this scene I'm thinking about—maybe cause I understood Romeo right down to his hot little bones—I got what they was saying pretty good. Except for this one part I'm still chewing on, like some kinda bone that ain't never gonna get eaten no matter how hard I bite down. Know what I mean, man, about things that should be easy as standing up but make you lose your balance every time and you just can't stop trying to do? It was funny how I could get that whole scene and couldn't figure that one line out, cause there weren't even no long Shakespeare words in it.

The day we got to that scene, it was snowing. It happens two or three times a year in the desert around El Chuco, man. The whole town comes to a standstill and nobody knows what to do except me. I was hypnotized, just standing there at the window of the classroom looking out at it.

I couldn't help it, man. I love it when it snows. Them flakes is the souls of every person that ever lived—even from the time of the cave people—floating to earth just to see what it feels like one more time. I go into a trance.

So I'm looking out at all them crystals of everybody coming back down to the ground and not noticing that everyone else is in their seats and Leila P. is burning holes in my back. Well, all of a sudden, I hear Miss Harper's scratchy voice—real sarcastic and breaking all rude into my dream of snow—"Somebody wake Louie up. I guess he's never seen snow." When I turned around—I took my time—everybody was laughing at me and Leila P. had this ugly look on her face like she hated them magic flakes.

Outta revenge, she made me and Marisa Pavane, the most beautiful girl in the class, who never talked to me, read our lines out loud. The wood-colored spool—that's Romeo, remember—was on the desk and the blue spool—for delicious Juliet—was on the cardboard platform above it. Maybe cause I was already in gagaland on accounta the snow, it seemed like I could see the real balcony and Juliet's hair, long and dark like Marisa's, while her and me read what we wrote down in our own words.

"And will you leave me here all hot and bothered?" I asked as Romeo, and some of the guys laughed real loud.

"Boys," old lady Harper said. "I know you can't help being your age, but please don't act like it." She was a killer, I tell you. "Go on, Marisa."

"How can I possibly satisfy you tonight?" Juliet asks in Marisa's words in a real innocent way and I know she is.

"By telling me you will only love *me*," Romeo answers through guess who. See? He was already wanting promises guys hafta have cause of their big egos. That's what I wrote down but I know how he really wants Juliet to satisfy him—only I can't say them words cause Miss Harper will get me thrown outta school.

But all the other guys, except Fernie Olivera, who ain't discovered what he's got between his legs yet, are looking at me and giving me a dirty smile cause they know, too. We're on to darling little Romeo and he ain't no saint. No teenage guy looking at a chick like Juliet ever was, let's be honest.

Juliet goes on. "I gave you my love before you asked me

for it. I wish it were still there so I could give it to you again."
Marisa was getting melodramatic cause all she ever bothered
to read careful was them comics about the lovelorn.

But Juliet knows about real love and her Romeo, like
Marisa, don't have no clue. All he wants to know next is if
Juliet is gonna take it away from him and if she is, how
come? Shakespeare knew guys. I know he did.

Juliet tries to explain it to him but Romeo ain't really
listening. He's looking at her where he shouldn't be looking
and wondering what he's gotta do or say to get what he
sees. Guys fall in love with their eyes, man, not their ears.
That's how come they can spend hours looking at pictures
of pretty girls without no clothes on.

It's the girls who have to hear a good line. That's how
come you see so many good-looking chicks with ugly, hairy
guys. Some of em even got hair growing outta their ears,
man, and wear lotsa gold chains. Them guys may look like
sleaze, but they got silver tongues, I bet you any amounta
money.

Then Juliet starts telling Romeo about giving love, her
kind of loving, and how she's already got all she's ever gonna
want and it goes on and on. The more she gives, the more she
has, til she's feeling like the whole ocean's inside of her. Even
then, I understood that much and wished for a woman like
Juliet cause then I could get it on with her every single night.

But that was where it came in, that line that I couldn't
figure out then and still can't. "And yet I wish but for the
thing I have." By then, Leila P. had both spools on the platform and told us to imagine that Juliet had her arms around
Romeo, which wasn't hard to picture cause that's what I
wanted to get to all along. But even thinking about them
finally making it didn't get me nowhere with that line. I still

162

didn't get it, and I raised my hand.

I could hear the flakes tapping against the window panes. Why them souls wanted to come into Miss Harper's classroom I'll never know. I sneaked a peek outside, and could see the snow falling and falling like mad. I wanted to be out there laying in the middle of the football field and letting em cover me up. You know, man, the way snow covers up plants to keep em from freezing to death. I'll never forget the first time I saw a snow-covered flower. It was one of them avocado moments.

"What is it, Louie?" Miss Harper asked in her tired-of-the-world voice.

"Well, Miss"—she hated it when we just called her "Miss" but this time she didn't even bother to correct me— "I don't get it. How can she wish for what she's got right in her arms? If she got it she don't need to want it." I knew I had her and Will good and that for once she wouldn't be able to explain away what was a mystery to me.

Leila P. looked at me harder than usual to make sure I was being serious and really wanted to know. It got real quiet—so quiet you could hear the snow falling on the window ledges, cause no one never dared interrupt Her Majesty like I done when she was in the middle of making us act out one of Will's scenes. But I couldn't help it. I had to know.

Then just when she looked like she was ready to wither me like she always done, her face did something real strange. The lines around her eyes and mouth went away and I could see that Leila P. had been young once, about ten thousand years ago. In a voice we hardly never heard from her, she said, "Have you ever been in love, Louie?"

"Sure," I lied. "Lotsa times."

I could tell she knew I was lying. A coupla girls made them nervous turkey noises and Leila P. whipped her head over and gave em a one-two punch with her eyes.

"Well, then," she said, all the wrinkles and a few more coming back into her face. "That line should make perfect sense to you."

She done it again, man, she played the old English teacher trick on me and was making me answer my own question! God! I hated that! She was the teacher, right? How come she couldn't just tell me? Her and Shakespeare, the perfect couple, guaranteed to drive you crazy worse than a horse on locoweed. How can anyone wish for what they already got and not be wacko bananas—maybe a good wacko, but still totally loco with no help in sight?

I looked out the window and the snow had stopped coming down. I knew it would all be melted by the time school got out and my heart sank. I knew Leila P. had made it stop with her hateful looks and was probably using her wooden leg like a wand to get it to melt so's she wouldn't have to look at it.

"Well, I still don't get it, Miss. I don't think you teach us too good." I slipped in that knife real easy.

"Well, then, Louie, you can just stay after school for an hour with me and we'll go over it together. Right now, I want to get through this scene without any more interruptions." She always got the last word, man, no matter what.

I stayed longer than an hour cause I wouldn't lie to her and tell her I understood that line. Finally, she let me go and told me that time would take care of it. I wanted to kick her in her real leg for that.

Time ain't done what she said yet, cause I still didn't get it thinking about that dumb line over and over in the car all the way down here. And I don't get it now neither, hearing it again and again all this time I'm talking to you. And I didn't get it this morning when I first got here and had to watch that buncha strangers in white take la Mollie away from me and roll her down what looked like the long dark corridor to forever. What am I gonna do, man? I'm crazy in love with her. There's gotta be a third act, right?

Can you tell me what them words are about, man, and what's gonna happen to my girl? You guys are supposed to know so much, do you know anything that can help me now? I coulda died myself when I had to hand la Mollie over to them white-coated butchers. I was standing there again in front of them big double doors that I just left a coupla hours ago—and now she's the one going inside where I don't know if I'm ever gonna see her again. And all I got for comfort is this line from the Avon man that I ain't never gonna make sense of—until I get interrupted by la Mollie's last words, which she left there hanging in the air for me to grab ahold of. And it's a good thing I know which words are real and which ain't.

"I love you, Clark," she told me.

I don't know if she meant Clark Gable or Clark Kent, man, or if she's thinking she's Scarlett or that wimpy newslady that's so hot to get into Superman's tights. But la Mollie was looking at me with one of them smiles of hers that made my heart do a Gene Kelly dance in the rain. She knows about me and the movies, so maybe it don't matter which of them heroes I get to play long as she's in the story with me.

And she don't bother to mention no Kahoutek killer comet, so maybe we all got a reprieve and are out on parole for a little while longer before we gotta shoot the last scene. Maybe talking to you is some kinda charm, man, like I been thinking sometimes, and all I gotta do to keep her alive is keep shooting off my mouth, til I'm sure it's gonna be her and me holding hands and taking that endless stroll into the desert sunset when the credits roll.

Whatever, I saw from her look that la Mollie could tell who she was talking to. Me, man. Chakespeare Louie, the baddest actor alive!

[AFTERWORD]

The Long Walk Home

by Paul Skenazy

I.

"You can go home again and again after and
if you are willing to grow up."
"On the Bridge, at the Border"

Arturo Islas was born in May, 1938, in El Paso, Texas. He
went to Stanford University in 1956, and graduated in 1960
with a degree in literature (he was one of only two non-
whites in his graduating class of more than a thousand).
He stayed on at Stanford to attend graduate school, left in
1964, and returned in 1968 to complete his studies. In
1970, he became a faculty member at Stanford, where he
won numerous awards for his teaching; he remained there
until his death in February, 1991, of complications from
AIDS. His two novels of the Angel family, *The Rain God*
and *Migrant Souls,* were published in 1984 and 1990, re-
spectively.

Louie Mendoza was born in September, 1986. Arturo
had just returned to El Paso to begin a one-year appoint-
ment to teach writing and literature at the University of
Texas, El Paso (UTEP). He moved into a bedroom at his
parents' house: "Arrange my room according to my taste—
all in order, rather pretty," he noted in his journal. He
obtained a key to the VIP room at the university library,
which was to serve as his study that year ("I love how
isolated it is"), and taught his first class on September 2.

As he records that day in his journal:

> An awful, terror-filled day. Unreality of my being here
> teaching. Students very badly prepared mostly . . . . Praying
> to be released of fear. Old, indescribable childhood kinds of
> September terrors. Inability to trust or have faith in anything.
> Mouthing prayers like a madman.

Insecurities about returning home lingered all year, but the "September terrors" quickly dissipated as he was claimed by his teaching and writing. One of the first assignments he gave his fiction class that September was to ask the students to write a story in a voice as unlike their usual style as they could imagine. When he did the assignment along with the students, Louie Mendoza started talking, and wouldn't stop.

On September 14, amid journal notations of phone calls to and from friends, visits with his brother and nephew, and a San Francisco Forty-Niners loss to the Los Angeles Rams, is this sentence: "Work on 'Kahoutek' in library." By the next day, he had ten pages of manuscript; less than a month later, the working title was "The Lame" and the story was more than fifty pages long. "I don't know where it's coming from, I just hope it keeps coming and coming," he wrote in his journal on October 6, a remark he was to echo in different ways throughout the next three months as Louie's tale emerged in an unprecedented rush. By mid-January, 1987, he was working on the ending:

> Came back to Mom and Dad's, drank a cup of coffee,
> went to my aerie and wrote the conclusion to "The Lame."
> I think it's going to be a lay down slam! Where is it coming
> from? I don't need/want to know.

Those initial renditions of Louie's story contain the essential events, most of the characters, and much of the commentary that make up the present novel. They partially survive in typescript. A very early eight-page version of "Kahoutek" tells about the coming of the comet, the arguments between Louie and la Mollie over Russian spirituality and the comet's fatality, Louie's horniness and his love of movies, the death of his daughter and his departure from El Paso, and it ends with Louie stalking out of the apartment. A slightly expanded version, still called "Kahoutek," includes Evelina's name and more about Louie's background, but still remains enclosed in the bedroom and kitchen. The 148-page typescript of "The Lame," on the other hand, is like the present novel in miniature. The scene is the emergency room of the hospital. Louie is recounting his long day with all its veiled premonitions. He walks us through San Francisco, describes events in the Park and at Big Eddie's, tells us about his struggles with Sonia and la Mollie, expounds on the wise and cranky Leila P. Harper and her buddy Shakespeare, and struggles to reach home only to return to the hospital in terror with la Mollie after her accident. The manuscript includes a couple of alternative versions of that "slam-bang" ending and, for the first time, contains a very shadowy prototype of the academic recorder, who has come to the emergency room along with a friend sometime early in the morning, and sits by Louie taking down all he says, for reasons unknown.

The subject of Kahoutek, linked to films, was one that had fascinated Arturo for some time in an offhand way. What has no reference before that September, 1986, is Louie Mendoza, whose existence seems directly linked to Arturo's first extended stay in El Paso since he left for college in 1956. Throughout his life, Arturo returned to El Paso several times a year for long visits, but 1986 was different. His

169

long-forsaken home town was a retreat where he hoped to find new foundations for his own confused life. He arrived both in triumph and despair, anxious about his future and excited by his work, curious whether the time had come to make his return more permanent. Louie Mendoza's existence clearly mirrors Arturo's own fascinated reentry into a world he had long deserted as his residence, passionately embraced as his imaginative and cultural home.

Although he wrote fiction constantly as a child, Arturo assumed that he would have a career as an academic critic. Then, in the early 1970s when a beloved uncle was brutally beaten, he took time to start writing about his family. Out of that writing grew his elegaic first novel, *The Rain God,* which recounts the fates of the "sinners" in the Angel family, a fictitious clan whose history owes much to the experiences of the Islases. The tales are recounted by Miguel Chico, who remains haunted by his childhood life growing up on the border, surrounded by the desert, and looks back to it balefully from his adult home in San Francisco.

Initial work on *The Rain God* was completed by 1974; ten years of frustration passed while Arturo struggled to interest a publisher—especially a New York publisher—in the novel. His rejection letters read like a course in Anglo stereotypes of Mexican Americans: There is not enough barrio life or violence in the novel; there is no reading public to buy the work of a Mexican American; the book lacks the voice of protest and political rage that should be part of any work from a so-called minority population. Arturo expressed his frustration in a letter that accompanied the manuscript in its rounds:

> Is there anyone in New York interested in good writing from a point of view that has not been given the exposure it

deserves?. . . There is a great need . . . for essays and fiction that speak to the concerns and lives of the *millions* of Americans of Mexican heritage. And we are not Blacks or Puerto Ricans or Cubans. Our experience and history, though similar in some general ways, has its own rich particularity. We did not cross an ocean to become Americans. In the southwestern parts of this country, we were here before the Anglo-Americans and European immigrant came on the scene. We are *migrants,* proud of our heritage and proud of our contributions to North American life. Why does the establishment continue to ignore us?

Finally in 1984 a small publisher in Palo Alto, Alexandrian Press, published *The Rain God.* Despite limited initial distribution, it was one of three nominees for the Bay Area Book Reviewer's Association (BABRA) Award for fiction, and it won the Southwest Book Award for fiction given by the Border Regional Library Association; in January, 1986, Arturo proudly returned to El Paso to accept the prize before his family and friends. Although ignored by the Eastern press, the novel gradually developed its own following, particularly on university campuses, and Alexandrian continued to reprint it over the next several years. Meanwhile, Arturo was at work on "A Perfectly Happy Family" (subsequently published as *Migrant Souls*), the next volume of what he imagined as an eventual trilogy about the Angel clan.

In 1985, Arturo came up for promotion to the rank of Professor at Stanford. Despite the anxiety he expressed in his journal that he was "gulled and unappreciated" by his colleagues, there proved to be almost unanimous support for his promotion. And in late September, 1986, just after his arrival in El Paso, a change of agents and a slightly altered atmosphere in New York resulted in the sale of

"A Perfectly Happy Family":

> 29 September: At about 3 P.M. [my agent] phones to tell
> me that she has sold my book to Morrow on the basis of
> one chapter for $15,000! . . . Oh, happy day!

So with his faculty position assured, *The Rain God* a success, and his second novel accepted for publication in New York as he had so long dreamed, Arturo entered his year at El Paso with a list of accomplishments that should have insured feelings of both security and satisfaction. But those old "childhood terrors" that he spoke of in his September journal entry remained. Like Miguel Chico in *The Rain God*, and Louie Mendoza in *La Mollie*, Arturo had migrated from El Paso long ago, leaving a residue of memory and ties too deep both culturally and personally ever to sever, yet also too binding emotionally to live with or within comfortably. He was a man of two worlds, two states, and multiple life-styles. Though he moved with grace and seeming ease between them, the strain showed itself in his immense insecurity, his drinking, and his cautions and suspicions amid the most intimate of friendships.

The 1980s also brought their own particular complications. The passionate love of Arturo's life was a man named Jay Spears. The two had been estranged for years, but Arturo was shaken in the fall of 1985 to hear that Jay had AIDS and was in the hospital. Over the next months, before Jay's death on December 5, 1986, the two men spoke and wrote frequently, and Arturo was quite moved by the deep reconciliation that occurred. He also was haunted throughout 1986 and 1987 by dreams of Jay, and his mourning was deep and unrelieved. He notes in his journal how he incorporates Jay's name into *La Mollie* in the figure of Virgil

172

Spears, and part of his pleasure with the ending to the novel comes from the fact that "I get to use J's line: 'And yet I wish but for the thing I have.'" Louie's relationship to la Mollie also mirrors much of the romance and tension of Arturo's own with Jay: the adoration of a blond, blue-eyed person from another class and ethnicity, raised in privilege.

In his journal, Arturo also looks back to the end of his relationship with Jay ten years before as the beginning of his heavy drinking. On January 28, 1985, on Colette's birthday (the one literary date Arturo mentions regularly in his journals), he went to his first AA meeting and gave up liquor. His entries for the next two years are filled with comments on AA meetings and worries about relapse. But on Colette's birthday in 1986, he looked back to his first twelve months of sobriety this way:

> A roller coaster year: reconciliation w/ Jay a miracle, even more the things he said to me; the move to El Paso; teaching @ UTEP; the Morrow contract; writing the entire Louie Mendoza section; Jay's death; the memorial service . . . not to have drunk for one whole year. Amazing and wonderful.

The El Paso stay from September 1986 to August 1987 proved to be an incredibly productive year. Arturo not only taught literature and writing courses, and conquered his drinking problems, but he completed drafts of *La Mollie and the King of Tears* and *Migrant Souls*. Still it was not an easy time. Journal entries record long lists of friends dying or dead from AIDS. With each sore or fever Arturo feared for his own health. He moved from joyful remarks about evenings visiting family or playing cards with his mother to angry reactions at family crises or age-old feuds that continued unabated. He was frustrated by the lack of interest in *La Mollie* by his editor while overcome by the gift of this new voice and angle on his fictitious worlds of El Paso and San Francisco. Long disassociated from the Catholic Church, he found new spiritual guidance through AA. And he struggled, too, trying to reconcile his positions as a gay man and Chicano writer:

> 25 May—The connection between my sexuality, which is private, and my tenuous (?) involvement with the Chicano community. I expect them to destroy me, at least to harm me in some way. I do not feel 'them' to be a source of emotional support. Much of my feeling can be traced to childhood terrors about being Mexican and about Mexicans. How easily, automatically, compulsively, I turn human beings, ideas, etc., into potentially harmful monsters. May this proclivity be taken from me Lord. I'm willing to live without that gun at the back of my head.

It is not hard to imagine that Louie Mendoza speaks from, and to, these paradoxes and irreconcilable confusions—the drinking, the "childhood terrors," the division between racial and sexual identity. And it seems clear that as Louie relates the story of his long walk home, he recounts the painful efforts Arturo himself made all his life to find his way back to himself—both who he might have been but wasn't, and who he had become in his long migration to and from this Texas-Mexico border world of El Paso.

II.

"There are certain dreams one pays for more
than others and the dream of romantic
love is the most expensive."

Journal entry, November, 1985

La Mollie and the King of Tears is the story of a day in July,
1973, when Kahoutek's path crosses the Earth's. On that
strange, seemingly fated day in Louie Mendoza's life, just
about everything goes wrong until he ends up in the emergency room with a cast on his leg awaiting word about la
Mollie's health and talking his way through the night and
morning to an unnamed academic who wanders in with a
tape recorder.

In a deeper sense, the story of that one day is the story
of Louie's whole life and how it has brought him to be as he
is, filled with the premonitions and hopes that he has—a
man whose allusions move from sweet breads and street
wars to the plays of Shakespeare. It is also, then, the story
of how he can be in love with a woman like la Mollie, so
different from him in education, class, and background, and
how he has become the sole figure of love in her life as well.
As Louie himself puts it: "That dumb comet was making
me look at things I ain't never seen or ever wanna see again."

What he sees, and helps us see, provides much of the
pleasure of overhearing his monologue. The separate elements that coalesce in the story are, as in most of Arturo's
writing, a compilation of observation, invention, and the
conjunction of experiences, some of which can be traced
back to their probable sources. In a note to himself on the
back of a page of manuscript, for example, Arturo says that
Leila P. Harper is based on two teachers from his high school
in El Paso. The image of the lawyer asphyxiated by heavy

chains repeats a similar scene in the fragmentary manuscript of *American Dreams and Fantasies,* the third volume of the Angel trilogy. A journal entry in 1986 about an AA meeting—"The 40 ft. pick-up truck doing donuts in his jail cell for 3 days"—turns into Louie's experiences trying to sober up under Teresa's and Manitas' watchful eyes. A friend's telephone report on a harrowing encounter with his wife— "[she] has gone berserk, hits him while he drives them on a windy road . . . tries to run him over, etc."—becomes a similar scene between Louie and la Mollie. And the moment when Louie recalls his dream of Evelina appearing to him in the arboretum at Golden Gate Park seems to emerge from December, 1986, when Arturo returned to San Francisco and went to the Park himself before attending the memorial service for Jay Spears: "Walk and tea in the Japanese gardens; then to the arboretum where I sit on the Joseph Agnelli bench in front of a pond and beyond a gingko takes me by surprise, as does its companion, a tulip tree in bloom."

Similar brief journal notations find their way into the novel—a talk by a colleague that prompts Arturo to see that the Chandos portrait of Shakespeare makes him look like a Chicano, a discovery at the Oriental Museum in Chicago about how they suck the brains from mummies. The figure of the Atomic "bi" man in the V.A. Hospital first appears in the manuscript after a trip Arturo took in the spring of 1987 through Los Angeles and New Mexico and incorporates journal notations of an overheard conversation, the names of an old Stanford classmate, and a man and his uncle who shine shoes.

The V.A. Hospital setting and the inspiration for Louie Mendoza's personality, on the other hand, come from Arturo's own years teaching educational therapy to war

veterans at a V.A. Hospital in Menlo park in the 1960s—
the same one, in fact, where Ken Kesey served as a nurse's
aide and which provided the model for the mental ward in
One Flew Over the Cuckoo's Nest. As Arturo explained
the experience:

> I taught there for three years, was almost fired for read-
> ing Bob Dylan lyrics in one of the classes, and learned much
> from the patients there, mostly how to talk to a group of
> people whose attention span is less than two minutes, cer-
> tainly not more than five. They were drugged most of the
> time, bitter, lonely, lost and absolutely forgotten. There was
> one psychiatrist for one hundred patients. They gave them
> cigarettes and Thorazine to keep them quiet.

And when Arturo wrote the assignment with his class that
September day in 1986, he thought back to a student in his
educational therapy class named Mr. Martínez who, as he
later remembered, "would respond in a thick Mexican accent, 'He's not here,' and mean it. Well, I guess in a way, he
wasn't, but in another way that would flourish many years
later, he was very much present."

These overt borrowings can only begin to suggest the
dense autobiographical underpinnig that this novel shares
with both *The Rain God* and *Migrant Souls,* and which is
apparent too in the obsessions and emotional concerns that
dominate all three works. Arturo himself clearly struggled
to construct overt links among the work: the introduction
of Miguel Chico as Mr. Angel, the teacher at the V.A. Hospital in *La Mollie,* for example, and the reference to Louie
inserted at the beginning of the second section of *Migrant
Souls,* when the sculptor Manitas de Oro, anxious to muster all the spirits he can to help retrieve the statue of Santa
Lucia, uses up "the entire box of incense that Louie Mendoza

had sent him from San Francisco during the hippie era."

More important than these formal ties is the fact that both Miguel Chico and Louie are figures embedded in San Francisco, inexorably linked to El Paso. Arturo's three novels share a dual focus on a lost and ghostly desert world of childhood that exists as a mute rebuke to a more crowded, more culturally confused adult California life. And in all three both the Texas-Mexican landscape and San Francisco reiterate similar preoccupations: oppositions of gender, class, sexuality, and race (people are threatened by and drawn to each other in their difference); cultural border crossings that need to be confronted daily; and an almost fatalistic testament to the way life insists people confront their own greatest fears and weaknesses. Both Miguel Chico and Louie struggle with pasts that are full of regret yet which they refuse to abandon because they are also the source of their spiritual strengths. And both men, for reasons at once distinct and parallel, struggle to stay afloat amid memories that threaten to drown them in feelings of obligation, guilt, and yearning.

One of the many things that sets *La Mollie* apart from the Angel fictions is the graphic details of San Francisco itself as a locale. Arturo's leap from the initial Kahoutek story to the novel came with the move out of la Mollie and Louie's apartment and into the streets, where Louie recounts his travels through the city's varied geography as a catalyst to his equally compelling journeys inside his memory; each step he takes across town catapults him back across time. The novel is embedded in the facts and sights, the traffic and neighborhoods, of 1970s San Francisco, from Golden Gate Park to the Castro, from the Mission district and Tommy's Joynt to the rich estates that line the waterfront. Louie's travels, and his yo-yoing memory, create a tale in

which we move absorbed in the cold and fogs of California, never too distant from the dry heat and desert harsh-
ness of El Paso—where the spiritual gurus of 1973 vie for
our attention with the Catholic priests of Louie's childhood.
And despite the nostalgia that permeates Louie's feelings
for his long-lost parents, it is clear that neither world provides a comfortable fit, nor prepares him for the assumptions or even vocabulary of the other. The way he presents
himself to us on the opening pages—his sexual deflation,
comments on the academic recorder, and brief asides on El
Paso—suggest a figure outside the parameters of Miguel
Chico's world with its burdens and blessings of an extended
family. For all the cacophony of voices that fill Louie's mind,
he is alone on his journey, an orphan looking for a place to
call home.

Louie's walks across town—to work during the day,
limping painfully home at night—serve as a metaphor for
the longer migratory journey of his life between scenes and
circumstances, worlds and languages: and for the longer
one so apparent in Arturo's own life as he negotiated his
ethnic heritage, his sexual desires, his illnesses, his education, and his cultural pleasures. Louie seems to represent
the Mexican American Arturo isn't, with entrance into yet
scornful of the world Arturo long inhabited. He is a for-
gotten, even forlorn, voice with which Arturo is speaking
to himself—a voice he is recovering and discovering at the
same moment. At once an outsider and insider, Arturo liked
clothes from Wilkes Bashford as much as la Mollie's friend
Bruce the lawyer does, and Louie's anger at such indulgence
seems propelled by self-contempt. Louie provides Arturo
with a caustic voice of self-scrutiny through which he can
portray himself as he might have been and was seen and

known by the street world of El Paso. *La Mollie,* then, becomes the world behind the looking glass of *The Rain God* and *Migrant Souls,* a way for Arturo to look not only at an alien world but at an alien (and alienated) self—overtly in portraits like those of the student at Stanford and of Mr. Angel at the V.A., covertly in the image of Tomás.

Arturo's own worried relationship to Louie is apparent in a preface to *La Mollie* he discarded shortly before his death, in which the novel is introduced as the purported transcript of a tape recording found among the papers of the late W. D. Higginson of San Cilantro Community College. A colleague of Professor Higginson explains that Louie's tale was recorded while the Professor was on sabbatical in San Francisco "pursuing his invaluable studies of the speech patterns of the underprivileged." Those studies, we're told, "drove him to unpleasant environments" where he "encountered *habitués* like the loquacious Mr. Mendoza, who spoke an unpolished language he sought to examine and explain to his students . . . ."

The preface goes on in this same vein, satirizing the language and posturing of the anthropological and sociological approaches to difference in which human beings are too often diminished into specimens of primitive tribal practices. This categorization of people into what in the academic jargon has come to be called the "Other" transforms individuals into informants we turn to for reports about life in the lower depths. Arturo's mockery of the pretentious academic language could not mask his bitterness at such an approach to Mexican American life because it not only dehumanizes the speaker but also scorns and appropriates the everyday speech of whole populations. Louie's comments on the way recordings steal words, and his plea for a definition of American speech inclusive enough to value a range of accents, are responses to the sense of exclusion that linguistic proprieties involve—as well, perhaps, as an admission of his own dependence on the recorder if he is to have his voice heard at all. The recorder's stance is a form of what Tom Wolfe once called "mau-mauing," and it is echoed elsewhere in *La Mollie* in the opera patrons who come to slum at Big Eddie's place, and in la Mollie's patronizing interest in Louie as a Noble Savage from El Paso who can provide firsthand information for her thesis.

It is to challenge that structure of reading and analysis that Louie himself speaks. In an interview published more than ten years ago, Arturo introduced us to Louie Mendoza long before Louie introduced himself to Arturo: "In the future there are going to be more and more good books by Chicanos, [and] . . . some of those books will be in a language that mixes standard English and Mexican Spanish and *calo,* barrio slang. That mix is as American as *Huck Finn.*" Louie Mendoza is a figure not only out of Mexican American life and the border world of El Paso, but a child, too, of America's long literary tradition that has glorified the voice, sensibility, and wisdom of the uneducated but street-wise observer as he casts a loving if skeptical eye on the presumptions of the powerful world around him.

If *The Rain God* owes its literary sensibility to the likes of Sherwood Anderson, Colette, Proust, and Henry James, *La Mollie* has more crude, arguably more adventurous, ancestors like Twain. In both *The Rain God* and *Migrant Souls,* characters must cope with being *mestizos,* or mixed bloods. While the Angel family—especially Mama Chona, the matriarch—insists that the children learn and speak a formal, traditional Spanish and value the Spanish heritage that links

181

them with Europe, the children themselves grow struggling to reconcile that class pride with their Indian heritage, the one Louie invokes early in *La Mollie* when he speaks of his Yaqui features and his mother's Olmec face.

Louie displays few doubts about his ancestry. He was born under the bridge that links, and separates, the United States and Mexico—born with little money to parents who would too soon disappear from his life if not his memory. But if his pride and self-assurance, his cunning and insecurity, begin under the shadow of that bridge, they more importantly take shape in his language. He claims to come not from El Paso, the border town discoverable on any map, but from El Chuco, the local slang term that develops into the word *pachuco*. Words and the mythological life embedded in them are Louie's lifeblood, and he seems, almost like Scheherazade, to live on his stories, inheritor of a tongue malleable enough to reinterpret Shakespeare, recall Hollywood films, roll his "r's" and drop his syllables. Like Huck Finn, his language distinguishes him from the society and social mores that surround him, while his ear for language and skills at mimicry allow him to absorb and take advantage of the speech patterns of others without succumbing to the cultural assumptions implicit in them.

Louie's dual role—at once our guide to and critic of San Francisco cultural life—is nowhere more apparent than in his raucous, insistent, insulting and charming voice. His voice is his distinction—his saxophone, if you will, with which he wails out the blues as he sits vigil over la Mollie. As claimant to the *pachuco* tradition—its zealous obsession with virility, its pride in its Mexican roots and derisive cynicism about United States values and virtues, its resistance to its own internal emotional sensibility—Louie is a narrative foil of extraordinary sensitivity. As we do with Huck Finn and other narrators who report clearly while at times unconscious of what they observe, and of their own best impulses, we see through Louie in both senses: out to the world around him, and into his complex internal contradictions and self-delusions.

And it is in Louie's language especially that we discover his masked tenderness, his incisiveness, and his incredible powers of reinvention. Louie mocks the student from El Paso he meets at Stanford with his tight pants and military shirt, he mocks Mr. Angel with his pretentious pronunciation and feminine mannerisms, and he mocks the high-mindedness of la Mollie and her friends. He especially rails against the self-aggrandizing and self-absorbed professionals with their institutional alliances: the historians who exclude whole populations from their stories, the priests who insult their congregations, the lawyers indifferent to justice, the doctors emphatically unconcerned about human suffering, the teachers who condescend to those they teach and the language their students speak.

But Louie, too, is finding his way among worlds, and he often proves to be no more graceful or forgivable in his task than those he scorns. For all his sarcasm, Louie wants into la Mollie's world. He describes his first weekend with her as the chance both to teach and hurt America for the way it has treated him, and (in an image reminiscent of a speech in Shakespeare's *The Comedy of Errors*) he imagines la Mollie's body as a cross-country map he journeys across. La Mollie's wealth and class work a contrapuntal melody to Louie's own poverty and racial standing, the two converging in the romantic plots of the films that act as leitmotifs throughout the novel. He feels, he says, like he's walking into a movie when he enters his life with la Mollie, and the star-laden series of film scenes he evokes while climbing the stairs to her at the end of his long journey makes it clear how completely she represents Hollywood happy-ever-after to him.

But it is in the arena of emotion, and in his range of emotional expression, that one feels Louie's deepest confusions, limits, and struggles. Louie can rarely express passion in any terms other than lust, save perhaps for the poetry that surfaces in his language when he talks about plants or about his music. Otherwise, the terms of desire are borrowed: from Shakespeare and Hollywood most often, from the clichés of pornography at other moments. And the frequency of his confessions about crying are only matched by the frequency of his apologies for his tears, as if feeling has no justification in his world. His training makes him masquerade behind mannerisms, care through his curses; like the "bi-" man, he is victimized by his dualism. He needs to begin his relationship with Virgil Spears with a fight and hide his affection from his gang, he struggles in shame with his tender concern for his brother Tomás and for Mr. Johnson at the V.A. Hospital, he disengages from his delight watching drag queens, he hides behind jokes when he finds himself aroused by Mr. Angel wearing a slip.

Louie's complex cultural negotiations are nowhere more apparent than in his contradictory reactions to the gay community that surrounds him. His insistent virility and tangled understanding of the nature of strength blinds him to his own impulses, and fears. At one point Louie realizes that we often hate the people we most resemble, but he never connects that insight with the (to him) confusing challenge he gets from the doorman at The Mind

Shaft that he needs to look at himself in the mirror to realize how we're all, gay or straight, just looking for our little brothers. While Louie advertises his sexual pleasures with such splendor, and professes a kind of homophobic obsession with women, he is constantly aware of and curious about men, and speaks of many, from his father and brother to Virgil, with deep affection. He reveals his immense sympathy for gays when he describes the self-flagellating passion that drives them to insert implements into their bodies or bind themselves in clothes pins and, however comically, it is gays Louie identifies with when he calls them romantics and idealists; it is not accidental that he himself is pejoratively called a "fag" by the PCP riders in the car on Market Street. In all these ways, he seems to fear an association with gays that both attracts and frightens him, and so exemplifies the tangled dilemmas Arturo also writes about in *American Dreams and Fantasies* when Miguel Chico claims that:

> none of us, no matter what the gender of the other, has any excuses: we are incapable of intimacy because we have been taught that self-possession is the highest masculine virtue. The cowboy rides alone.

On the other hand, there is the penetration of Louie's slang; his voice is his redemption, even for readers who might sometimes grow weary of his frequently reductionist vocabulary, his insolent self-delusions, and his tough-guy pretensions. Words and talk are both a drug and an antidote for Louie, a symptom of illness and a form of cure. They help him recognize, place, and proclaim himself, and also avoid himself. As a narrative device, Louie's talk binds together the episodic and associative jumps between past and present, but they also seem to bind his spirit together as well. Memory revives and restores Louie, often literally allowing him to move on from one place to another. His memories and allusions to Shakespeare and films are his crutch, helping him walk through an alley, understand a remark, climb the stairs, maintain his self-confidence in the face of despair. He is a figure who constantly rebuilds himself by reacquiring the past as he walks across the city and through time, learning about his capacities to love and mourn and worry his way home as he goes. And behind all the words too comes an unaskable series of questions: can his talking help cure la Mollie, or at least keep her alive—in a metaphorical sense, can his story somehow revive her? And if it can't, then are all the words in the world worth anything? Does what we do ever add up to much, if it can't save those we love? Do the reels of tape that contain his voice, his story, and hence his life, accumulate into something significant?

But the uncertainties that punctuate Louie's remarks are more than offset by the energy and delight that pours out of him in his endless stream of judgments, memories, and comments. His attitudes are a mix of the delusions of ordinary public opinion and the wisdoms learned in the school of hard knocks. There is nothing simple in Louie's cultural position, and it is just as impossible to dismiss him as an uneducated *pachuco* as it is to turn him into a wise visionary. He is someone who often is unaware of his own best gestures, who negates his deepest goodness, yet who knows something of the minute pleasures of plants and the intimacies of friendship.

As we begin to realize how for Louie life and language are all but equated, how to speak out is to re-create oneself word by unmeasured word, his position in relation to the academic recorder becomes that much more complex and interesting, and dangerous. The interview that comprises the book is on the one hand an acknowledgment on the academic's part of Louie's existence and importance, on the other a dismissal of his story to a category of accent and syntactic variation. Louie himself, on the other hand, speaks for an equality of voice and point of view in his comments on the language of the heart, his insistence on the multiple languages and lives that make up the American culture, and his opposition to the false words and claims of history, psychology, and the insights of scholars. Louie's insistent declamation through storytelling, his poses and constant process of self-revision, and the discordant sound of his swearing and rages serve as a resistance to propriety, a reminder of the everyday that stands in contrast to the false, unreal verbiage of the lawyer, the priest, the doctor, or the academic. Yet all his statements are only preserved because of the recorder and his academically invested power to make this record of the night—a man of authority who cannot understand Louie's barrio slang and who Louie must call on frequently for confirmation that anything about his point of view has gotten through.

Nowhere is this complex pattern of reinvention through self-proclamation, and dependence on the authority of others to be heard, more beautifully realized than in Louie's thoughts about his former teacher, Leila P. Harper, and her efforts to teach him Shakespeare. Miss Harper is the one teacher in Louie's life, it seems, who took him seriously enough to fight with him, demand attention of him, resist him, and offer him a world so entirely outside himself that he can understand himself through it—and he repays her by becoming both her nemesis and her protégé. As her finest student, Louie affirms the cultural point that different ways of seeing often merge and converge if each is given credit by the others. His understanding of Shakespeare's plays provides a classic example of the kinds of recombinations and restatements so characteristic of a multicultural border world, where new meanings are negotiated by curious and surprising borrowings, joinings and clashes of disparate sources. Louie can view Shakespeare with suspicion, and, by testing the plays against his own experience, learn something from the Bard as he instructs us anew in Shakespeare's wisdoms; the plays are universalized by being localized.

Thus Louie's relations to Miss Harper and Shakespeare involve not only a relation to language but to ideas of what culture is, how it is understood, where it helps one position oneself in the world. Like the films Louie constantly alludes to, Shakespeare offers parallels and validations, provides Louie with the opportunity to examine and comment on his life and world in a broader context. Unlike films, Shakespeare's dramas are a form of art that Louie claims not to understand well or model himself on at all, though even with films Louie is less given to interpretation than acquisition: an extraction of those parts that interest him. And despite all of Louie's confusion about Shakespeare's meaning, he never accuses the Bard of falsifying the world. Instead he realizes, sometimes despite himself, that like his beloved films and music, Shakespeare offers insights he can depend on. In this way, his interaction with Shakespeare can stand for the broader intersection of Chicano border life with America's European inheritance. Arturo often described himself as living "on the bridge, at the border" of worlds, and the year before he died gave a lecture with that title. *La Mollie* also exemplifies this stance of living stationed between worlds and cultures, nowhere more than in Louie's interactions with Shakespeare's legacy.

The novel is intensely shaped by Shakespeare. This is not only true in the smaller motifs, as when Louie comments directly on Hamlet and his mother, Macbeth's struggles with power and corruption, Lear's blind love and inconsolable mourning, or Romeo's horniness and Juliet's passion. But the book as a whole is shaped as an open-ended meditation, a kind of slang footnote or exegesis, on the romance of Romeo and Juliet, the actions of two immature lovers contemplating loss. However often Louie claims ignorance about Shakespeare's meanings, Arturo insists that the reader recognize Louie's spirited insights, be they displayed through Louie's actions or in those offhand asides of his that so often carry significant moral weight. This is particularly true of Louie's wisdom about the refrain that echoes through the story, "And yet I wish but for the thing I have." We see this idea again and again in Louie's narrative of his life, as his mind and memory swing from Sonia to la Mollie, Tomás to la Pixie, the pot-of-gold man to his father. The thing we most value, the thing we are most blind to, the thing we struggle to claim as our own because we remain unrelentingly unable to recognize that we already possess it: these are the patterns Louie reports, recognizes, repeats, relives as he retells his long, long day and night under Kahoutek's flaming shadow. And as he bestows that day on us, we too come to learn about the buried lives we all possess and undervalue, whether they be the flowers and trees of Golden Gate Park, the love of a woman, a memory of a lost daughter, the sound of a piece of music, a repeated line of Shakespeare—or a lover who has just died of AIDS.

La Mollie and the King of Tears is a novel of shifting times, alternative spaces. It describes a post-hippie, pre-AIDS world where drugs and drink play casually through the atmosphere, where psychological cures are rampant—a world that is sexually liberated if also tangled in its own hedonism. But a third time also shades the novel: the post-AIDS moment of its creation, in 1986 and 1987. Our knowledge of that impending world, and the narrative's resistance to it in the leap backwards to 1973, account for many of the tensions and contradictions about sex roles that are so apparent in Louie's comments on himself and his brother Tomás. The smallest references—to Rock Hudson in a film, for example—are freighted not only reading the novel now, in our present atmosphere, but as Arturo himself was writing. Opening the book is like reading a map with historical overlays, transparencies of time and experience that insist we view the culture's self-description with the hindsight of the historian who sadly recognizes both a flamboyant and disease-laden moment.

Perhaps this 1980s focus helps us to understand the extraordinary mixture of wild energy and pleasure in life, and the frantic, almost fatalistic terror of impending doom, that are so much a part of Louie. Arturo's first novel, *The Rain God,* begins with an operation for a colostomy and ends in a vision of the Angel family, along with the family ghosts, standing at the matriarch, Mama Chona's, deathbed. Though resistant to the poetic and lyrical turns and the tragic tone of *The Rain God, La Mollie and the King of Tears* is set in a hospital, at the verge of death. Arturo's own life, from his polio attack at the age of eight through a colostomy in the early 1970s and to his death in 1991, was also lived hovering between physical beauty and deterioration.

In such a framework of disease and disability, the working title of the novel—"The Lame"—is both suggestive and descriptive. Louie is not the only character who limps through life—there is Big Eddie's manipulative cane, for example, and Leila P. Harper's wooden leg. More metaphorically, there is the deformed hunchback tree Louie hugs for dear life. Almost all the characters have their gimpy appendages, physical and psychological—the men in the V.A. Hospital with their half-faces and dual personalities, their disregard for history and drooling indifference to speech; Evelina in her visionary insulation; la Mollie with her head wound, mental debilitation, and displaced identity; Mr. Angel with his limp (Arturo himself walked with a limp from his childhood polio).

Within a life that was too often a kind of ongoing emergency room of the spirit, Arturo discovered his vocation as a writer, worked at his craft, and found the generous and life-affirming energy that one feels channeled into Louie's slangy kindness. Louie's story might have begun as the effort to find an alter-ego, a voice opposite Arturo's own, but it soon became an expansion and rediscovery of the self— an opportunity to examine buried, suppressed, unexercised lives and thoughts. It is as if in opening himself to a voice like Louie's Arturo assumed the uncomfortable role of the unnamed academic recorder of Louie's confession, challenged to recognize his affiliation and even blood connections with this seeming stranger. This is the Other turned on its ear, turned inward—not so much absorbed by the self as rediscovered as a neglected part of oneself—as another, unknown but not uninteresting and no longer repellent self.

In the surviving fragment from *American Dreams and Fantasies*, Miguel Chico argues that the message of the New Testament seems lost to most in American society: 'Love thy neighbor as thyself' *No exceptions*. It is the greatest, most difficult, imaginative concern in all of western literature.

In this context, the recorder—so unknowing yet forever listening—serves as a stand-in for us all as readers. Louie's responses to him—his confessional insistence, his challenges about motive, his arguments with the limits of the recorder's training, language skills, and sympathy—are challenges to us all as interlopers on his unknown life. (It is not only Louie who is the Other here, but la Mollie who serves that role for him as well.) The book itself becomes a plea for recognition that challenges us to honor Louie's voice as one with our own in its distinctiveness, its inconsistencies and contradictions, its coarse humor, its frustrations and longings. Our attention to the book is our acknowledgment of the speaker, our recognition of his claims to our attention.

III.

"I would have liked more time to learn to write, to keep learning how to do it . . . because it's never a finished thing . . . ."

Arturo Islas, in an interview
with José Antonio Burciaga

Even as Arturo was completing a draft of "The Lame" in January, 1987, he worried about the reception it might have: "Continuing thoughts that no one but me will care about L. Mendoza." But when she read it, Arturo's agent was enthusiastic, suggesting that it, rather than "A Perfectly Happy

Family," might serve as his New York debut. He sent it off to his editor with fear and determination: "Oh, God, I hope she likes it as much as I because I will fight hard for it!" She didn't, at all, and he put aside Louie Mendoza's story for much of that spring to return to the Angel family, anxious to complete what was to become *Migrant Souls* for a December deadline. He continued to think about "The Lame," however, reading portions of it to audiences—at a high school, for example, he notes that "the students liked it; the elders frown on Louie Mendoza"—and reworking the early scene about Louie and Macbeth into a short story (it appeared as "Chakespeare Louie" in *ZYZZYVA*).

Early that summer, he shifted back to " The Lame," and again the material came to him at what he could only describe as an "uncanny" pace. He added several scenes one finds in nascent form in his journal. He tried out alternative titles—"Chakespeare and the Barrio," "The King of Tears"—on his agent, and she suggested a third variation: *La Mollie and the King of Tears.* Near the end of June that year, he noted: "Still putting finishing touches on Louie Mendoza. I can feel that I'm tiring of him and my imagination is aching for something else. That's good!"

Arturo completed revisions on *La Mollie* shortly after his return home to Palo Alto, California, that August and he began showing the completed manuscript to people at Stanford—somewhat apprehensively, it appears. He bristles, for example, when two close friends respond, to his eyes, "guardedly": "Unless I am misinterpreting—they. . . do *not* like what I've done. I'm steady about that, though I have a few moments of feeling intensely defensive. How sheltered they keep themselves! I ain't no nice Mexican altar boy any more and *that* scares them."

193

But health matters more and more came to preoccupy him in the fall of 1987. Longer and longer lists of acquaintances and close friends now dead or suffering from AIDS appear periodically in the journal, along with comments about their heroism and equanimity in the face of death. He speculates, too, about his own strength to encounter his mortality as he notes each outbreak of herpes, each chancre sore or infection.

And then, in January, 1988, Arturo discovered that he was HIV-positive. Months of depression and thoughts of suicide followed; a year later he was in the hospital with pneumonia, and he had lost fifty pounds. His journal for 1988 is filled with fears that each visit with his family might be his last, and he grew more and more anxious about his ability to muster the time and energy to see his novels in print. He sent *La Mollie* to several publishers, but no one was interested.

Migrant Souls was published in the winter of 1990, and the reviews, though mixed, crushed Arturo. He felt the comments on the novel were shallow and short-sighted. He was frustrated and disillusioned by what he saw as a lack of effective publicity from the publisher, and by some of the editorial decisions he had permitted in the revision process. He was upset when his work was ignored in a survey article on recent Chicano writing that appeared in the *New York Times* and disturbed by what he saw as the two-faced opportunism of many: reviewers who would compliment him to his face and slur him in print, editors who made offhand remarks he found insensitive and bordering on racist. He was also both delighted and, admittedly, jealous of the reception garnered that year by Oscar Hijuelos' *The Mambo Kings Play Songs of Love,* while his own jazz musician Louie

Mendoza played solo in a desk drawer. He was raging not only against the New York establishment, but his own fate: his exhaustion and ill-health just as he was most engaged in his fiction—the work undone, the fame ungarnered.

The year had been filled, too, with rejection letters from publishers for *La Mollie,* and as Arturo's health deteriorated, and the work he had hoped to do remained undone, he grew more and more despondent. The fact that at the same time he signed a contract with Avon to republish both *The Rain God* and *Migrant Souls* in paperback, and that he participated in two major conferences with Latin American writers who respected and praised his work, buoyed his spirits considerably, but did little to lighten his gloom about the responses to *La Mollie.*

By the summer of 1990, Arturo was tired, unable to work for sustained periods, fighting frequent illnesses and carefully regulating his public time. A flu in early July turned worse and worse, and by the end of that month he weighed only 120 pounds and was completely dehydrated before his health took a brief turn for the better. He continued to accept invitations to read from his work, continued to travel to and from El Paso to see his family, continued his intimate phone and visiting relations with his large number of close friends around the country. He continued to remain sober, too, taking solace in the meetings and companionship offered by AA.

Arturo remained devoted to *La Mollie* and surprised that others did not share his enthusiasm. Although I had read and taught "Chakespeare Louie" and had heard Arturo read from other sections of the novel, it was only during that summer of 1990 that I first read the book from start to finish. I went to his home frequently after that throughout the late summer and into that fall where, amid our more general exchanges of gossip and jokes, we talked over the manuscript and ideas about revision.

Arturo phoned me in February, 1991, the night before he died, to ask me to collect the manuscript of *La Mollie,* find a publisher, and work through the necessary revisions to prepare it for publication. "Get Louie out, Paul," he insisted, "they'll love him." By "they" he meant that anonymous but broad public he always knew was available for works like his, a public he felt he'd too often been separated from by publishers' assumptions rather than actual reader predilections or tastes.

In the years since Arturo's death, I've worked to try to fulfill that claim Arturo made on our friendship. The published novel that you have in your hands is the novel Arturo wrote, yet on almost every page it differs slightly from the manuscript I picked up from him the next morning. Excisions have been made to assure that all the incidents of the original appear here, if sometimes in condensed form. *La Mollie* is like a shaggy dog story, a kind of suspended moment that is held, reiterated, and refined while the elements that comprise that moment accumulate to enrich its significance. The forward movement of the book is backwards: into remembrance, association, explanation, intensification. It is, in many ways, a book without a conclusion, or with the ostensibly central issue of la Mollie's health suspended still even in the last words. Though by the end we know so much more about Louie, and a little more about la Mollie, we remain as uncertain as Louie himself whether she will live or die.

That kind of suspended plot requires a continuous, rapid inventiveness and a coordination of scenes so that we move comfortably if at times suddenly between memories of the past, the events of the day, and Louie's retrospective comments as he recounts his experiences to the recorder. Arturo himself knew that work needed to be done to rethink certain moments and to coordinate the various episodes of memory, dream, and allusion. He had begun, if only begun, the process of revision. Some sections, particularly the first two chapters, were more polished than others. There were imbalances apparent in the novel that had to be rectified: scenes needed to be shortened, sometimes shifted in relation to each other. Certain characters were undeveloped, certain references were inconsistent.

In all these, I served, not always comfortably, as Arturo's stand-in, moving from decision to decision on the basis of the small number of corrections and revisions Arturo himself had time to complete before his death, our conversations about other scenes and characters, our talks about Louie and his background (and Arturo's own, on which much of it was based), and my knowledge of Arturo's other works. Each page was reviewed, each line examined, in the effort to make the book the story Arturo had to tell. Certain areas of the novel, particularly the significant relationship between Louie and the unnamed and unvoiced (but frequently tartly rendered) recorder of Louie's words, have been intensified in conjunction with Arturo's plans and in line with the discarded preface. No new characters were invented, no new scenes imagined. And of course, most important, all efforts have been made to maintain the voice of Louie Mendoza, who is the key—indeed, the body—of this book.

In an interview with José Antonio Burciaga shortly before he died, Arturo talked about how fiction helps create the shape of life.

197

Life has no shape. We impose shape on it so that we can deal with it. It's so scary to think that it's all chaos. And what artists do to the *n*th degree, what writers do to the *n*th degree, without seeming to do it—this is the trick, you see—is to give shape to things that have no shape. The human heart has no shape. Emotions have no shape . . . . I'm still learning how to write a novel . . . I wish I had more time. I wish I hadn't started so late to write. But I didn't know I was going to write . . . . I guess I am grateful for what I have written, but . . . I got started real late and I'm not going to have time to complete.

Like la Mollie's fate, the book that bears her name will remain forever incomplete. That incompleteness, however, is similar to Louie's unfinished pondering of the line from *Romeo and Juliet* that echoes through the final scenes: "And yet I wish but for the thing I have." As that line hovered over Arturo during the writing, reflecting his own lost love, so it hovers over Louie in his waiting, speaking to the incomplete fulfillments we all grapple with in this earthly life. My hope is that however incomplete *La Mollie and the King of Tears* remains, it too will give new meaning to that experience of love, of injury, and of worry, where we struggle, often against ourselves, to find our way home. For in that journey we, like Louie, are left to weigh the unclear messages that are often all we have, and to look forward, however apprehensively, to the uncertain mystery of our being just who we are.

[ACKNOWLEDGMENTS]

The process of bringing *La Mollie and the King of Tears* to publication has involved a number of people and a number of steps. My dear friend Don Rothman read and reread the manuscript and offered invaluable help and comments. Arturo's literary executor, Diane Middlebrook, read the manuscript and afterword at key phases, and provided me with valuable personal information about Arturo's whereabouts and state of mind during his year in El Paso. Poet and novelist Benjamin Sáenz, a former student of Arturo's, first made the connection with the patient and generous people at Broken Moon Press in Seattle, Washington, where this book was, originally, nurtured for publication under the patient and generous eye of publisher Lesley Link until the press itself ceased operation in 1995. Mary Helen Clarke, the book's editor at Broken Moon, worked closely with me and proved a sensitive and suggestive reader. When Broken Moon released the manuscript, I approached Beth Hadas, director of the University of New Mexico Press, who took on the roles of editor and publisher with great enthusiasm, and she and her production staff at UNM have been wonderful in their commitment to the novel.

About the Author

Arturo Islas was born in El Paso, Texas. He earned his undergraduate, graduate, and doctoral degrees from Stanford University, where he continued as a professor of English. He was a member of Phi Beta Kappa, a Woodrow Wilson Fellow, and a University Fellow, as well as a recipient of the Lloyd W. Dinkenspiel Award for outstanding service to undergraduate education. His previous novels, *The Rain God* (Avon, 1991) and *Migrant Souls* (Avon, 1991), were acclaimed and won several prizes. Shortly before his death of AIDS in 1991, Islas was named to the El Paso Writers' Hall of Fame.